Music from another Country

⌘ *Music from another Country*

Music from another Country

Jeremy Fisher

Fat Frog Books
Sydney

Music from another Country

First published 2009 by
Fat Frog Books
49 Northcote Street
Haberfield, NSW 2045, Australia.

Contact the author through the Australian Society of Authors, PO Box 1566, Strawberry Hills, NSW 2012. Ph: 612-9318-0877. Email:asa@asauthors.org

For
Allan Fisher
DFC
1921–2001

Back cover photograph: Jill Dimond

Printed in the United States of America by lulu.com

National Library of Australia CIP Data available

Fisher, Jeremy

Music from another Country / Jeremy Fisher

ISBN 978-1-4092-8416-1

Thursday, July 29, 1943
Remscheid, Germany
11:37 p.m.

He wanted to piss. He needed to piss. There was an L-san toilet down the back of the plane, past the bomb bay and over the main spar. But he couldn't leave his position. They were too close to target. The pathfinders had lit the first flares.

He wriggled in his seat and tried to push his knees together as much as the flying suit would allow. His bladder felt no relief. He and the flight engineer had rigged up a tube attached to a bottle to pee into when they couldn't leave their places in the cockpit of the big bomber. He couldn't reach for that. He couldn't release his thickly gloved hands from the joystick yet. The whole squadron was in position, a tight wedge of Lancasters in the black German night sky. Each plane packed with tons of bombs ready for release into the darkness. The flares were now guiding them directly to the black spot beneath them which would soon erupt into a firestorm. And he wanted to piss.

Three minutes to target. Remscheid. He had never heard of the place before the briefing at Waddington some hours before. The English officer who had briefed them had made quite a thing of pronouncing the city's name, rolling his plummy accent over the "Rem" and hissing the "scheid".

"'Scheid' like in 'height' for all you colonials who don't know German," he'd said. Even though this was an Australian squadron, many of the aircrew had been seconded from the RAF. The hierarchy of empire had been seconded with them. "Remscheid. Near Dusseldorf. A fair-sized place. Makes some ball bearings and other mechanical stuff for the Nazis. But tonight the time has come for Remscheid to pay for its place in the Nazi war machine. We are going to hit it, and hit it hard."

The crews had checked their charts over mugs of tea, then gathered into their own groups of seven. The squadron assembled outside in the warm English evening, kitted up and ready for the truck which would ferry them out to their planes. The leather flying jackets and the flying suits were too hot for ground level, but they would be needed once the unpressurised Lancasters reached their maximum altitude. Neil Piggott was Flight-Sergeant, and pilot. By regulation he had to wear his parachute in a pack under his bum. He sat on it in his cockpit seat. Beside him sat Bill, his flight engineer, who looked after the many mechanical and technical advantages of the four-engined plane. These big birds were too much for a pilot to handle every detail. Bill, his flight engineer could handle the plane in flight, too, but not for take-offs and landings. Behind and below the cockpit, in a well in the plane, the Navigator had his position. He took readings with his sextant, checked the new instruments which were being installed all the time as the boffins came up with new ways to make night bombing more accurate, and followed the readings and signals sent out by the pathfinders, the loners whose dangerous responsibility it was to identify then light up a path to the targets.

A new instrument had just been installed in the plane. It was Gee. The receiver on the plane took short wave signals from ground stations. The boffins had said that by measuring the time taken between the arrival of the pulses, the Navigator could accurately chart his plane's position. The Navigator shared his space with the Wireless Operator, whose job it was to monitor the airwaves, as generally they flew in silence. He would broadcast signals to try to jam enemy communications. He also operated the forward guns. Amidships, the mid upper gunner peered out from his little bubble into the blackness of an alien night. Further back, right at the tail of the plane, the rear gunner manned his distant position. He flew backwards, exposed in his turret. The last member of the crew was the bomb aimer, whose active position was prone underneath the cockpit. There, he could monitor the plane's progress through his sights, and ensure the bombs were released as close to target as the rapidly developing technology of war allowed.

Hours before, they had boarded the plane, and the squadron had left its English base in tight formation. Now searchlights fingered up at the squadron, none of whom he could see in the otherwise pitch black. A shaft of light hit them, was gone, then back. Other fingers of light quickly moved to converge. They had been coned. Base had said the Germans were using radar now to target their searchlights. Two minutes twenty seconds to target. Jesus Christ, now they were the target! A flash to starboard showed they were in some gunner's range. The radar story might be true of the guns too.

"Holy Mary Mother of God get us out of here," his rear gunner suddenly screamed through the intercom. The big plane shuddered as ack-ack exploded near, but he held it on course. "Did you hear me Skipper?" The rear gunner had been talking most of the trip. He was making less and less sense. It sounded as though he was not getting enough oxygen. There had been some faults in the bottles each crew member was supplied with. Something would have to be done as soon as the bombs were away.

"I have the target flare in view," the bomb aimer came through, calm and detached. "Half a degree to port, Skipper."

"Begging your pardon, Skipper, but every bloody Remscheider can see me hanging out my washing here." The rear gunner again. "There's more light back here than at bloody noon on Bondi Beach. Please get us out of here now." Keep silent, Dusty. Panic quietly. It was extremely lonely down the tail end. Dusty would be peering out into a nothingness of exploding flak and stabbing searchlights, a lack of vital oxygen intensifying his fears. Even without that, he was cracking a little more each mission. Another burst of ack-ack. Closer. Some hit them. Even with the earphones on he could hear the thumps. And some clattering, just like stones on a metal roof. He could feel the force of the hits through the joystick. But still he held the Lancaster on course.

The big plane shook as an accurate volley of ground fire ripped through the starboard wing. More fingers of light began to twist through the night's blackness towards the plane. Air defence would be after them soon. A Messerschmidt on their tail, or underneath, and they were gone. The Lancaster was especially vulnerable to fighter attack.

One minute forty seconds to target.

"One degree to starboard," the bomb aimer barked over the intercom from his little nest below the pilots. The intercom was silent now, the rest of the six crew leaving all direction to the bomb aimer for the few minutes until they reached the target.

There was a burst of fire from the mid-upper gunner. Nothing to indicate what he was shooting at. Then kerump. Kerump. Kerump. Kerump. Closer and closer up the fuselage, as tracer hit them. "Number three's bought it." Neil's flight engineer immediately reached up to hit the feathering button, routine providing a welcome diversion. Out on the wing a brief flurry of flames gave some indication of the damage, then the darkness cloaked them again. Now all of the crew were talking. Neil could hear the staticky voices of his crew members, calming each other across the intercom.

"Quiet," he growled to them.

Then they were alone in the sky with the music of their flying machine. The throb and hum of the engines reached throughout the plane. The straining whistle from the open bomb bay scraped an off-key note, just as the bomb bay doors scraped against the plane's airflow and forced Neil to hold the plane on course. An ever-present white noise over which little beats and percussions played, some, like the tracer, louder than others. It was this rhythm he rode, his hands in their thick flying gloves reading the pulsations and stresses of the plane, intuitively reacting to each bang and shake to keep the big bird on course.

"Thirty seconds to target," the bomb aimer's calm voice announced. "Twenty." Neil tightened his grip on the joystick as another stream of tracer crashed into the fuselage. "Ten." He could see a thread of bombs exploding below them, indication that a luckier member of the squadron had already found the target. "Bombs away."

The plane rocked and floated up as the weight of the bombs left its belly. Neil immediately threw the bomber into a dive, with a sharp turn to starboard. He levelled out briefly before pitching to port in a climb. He'd managed to throw off some of the searchlights, but two still held them. He corkscrewed the plane, turning it hard aport. He dived 400 feet, then straightened and levelled. Now he was pushing the bird as hard as he could with only three engines turning. But they had lost the searchlight. They dropped five thousand feet. He flew on in darkness for a few minutes, zigzagging in a general course towards the coast. No fighter appeared.

He needed to piss. He was going to have to go. He looked across at Bill. He was staring dead ahead, his face, usually pallid where it was not hidden by the oxygen mask, drained now of all colour. There was a wash of sweat all over him, even though the plane was 18,000 feet up and the cabin temperature below zero. "Bill, can you take her. I've got to have a leak," Neil spoke into the intercom. Bill turned to give him a brief, terror-struck look, but he took the controls. Neil briefly considered switching on the autopilot instead, Bill being so frightened of control, but it wouldn't have responded quickly to any emergency. He unclipped his own oxygen mask, and reached back for the tube and bottle with as much haste as he could with the gloves. He struggled the gloves off and unzipped his flying suit enough to extract his penis from the mandatory longjohns he wore under his uniform. The air was so cold there was not much of it to grab. He pissed a long stream into the rubber tube he and Bill had contrived for these difficult occasions, the steam rising. Pissing was one of the most difficult of all the tasks a bomber pilot had to perform. Though not always confined to his seat, always there were layers of clothing he had to get through. These night runs were bad enough when everything worked. Being able to piss like this was an extra convenience they had made for themselves. It wasn't regulations, this device, but it was one of their few comforts. Midstream, he felt a punch, punch, punch hitting the plane. A glance at Bill told him his flight engineer had lost it, this sudden attack sending him that little bit further and over the edge. Bill was not a pilot, though he could hold the plane on course when necessary. Now he had shoved the plane into a climb, oblivious to the altimeter's reading. If there was a fighter on their tail, this was madness. They had to dive, and in the darkness somehow try and find cloud cover.

Neil couldn't stop the flow of urine out of him. The piss continued, steam flowing from the tube and bottle. "Port!" Neil yelled. "Turn to port, then dive." His yell was useless without the intercom. The flow began to ease, but Bill was acting with agonising slowness. Neil tossed the tube and bottle behind him. Unseen, behind and below him, the yellow liquid began to flow into the fuselage of the plane, close to the well where Jack, the navigator, and the wireless operator crouched uncomfortably in their small space. It trickled down to freeze around their boots.

Neil clipped his oxygen mask and intercom back on. "I'm taking her," Neil shouted into the intercom. He pushed forward on the stick, and the plane nosed into a dive. Tracer shells streamed harmlessly past them, a ribbon of fire fading into the night.

He pushed forward, diving even more steeply. He couldn't outfly an Me109, but maybe they were lucky and they'd just crossed the path of a slower Dornier. At 10,000 feet, he levelled out the plane then turned it ninety degrees to starboard. Heavy blasts rocked the starboard wing. Instantly, he noticed a loss of power in the number two engine. Firing like that would have to be from a fighter. Luck was not with them. More firing. An explosion. "Oh Christ." The mid-upper gunner. Bill was screaming, "God, Skipper, that's done it. We're not going to make it. We're going to have to bale out."

"No! Get the extinguishers! Put out that fire!" He could hear but not see the fire amidships. Bill sat for a second, stunned at Neil's order. Then he unbuckled himself and lurched down towards the flames.

"I can hear him!" the wireless operator yelled. "I'm going to try to jam the bastard."

"Anything," Neil answered. Neil had levelled out again, and now he turned the plane ninety degrees to port to make targeting as difficult as possible for any fighter in pursuit. But with the light coming from the fires, it would be almost impossible for anyone to miss them. Smoke had come into the cockpit. Thick, black and acrid. "We're going to get back," Neil whispered, too quietly for the intercom to pick it up. His hands were tightly gripping the stick, awash with sweat inside the thick leather flying gloves. He was sweating all over, the wool lined flying boots soaking wet.

He squinted into the darkness, less smoke oozing up around him as the fires were smothered with foam. The creeping bubbles of foam were like the warm, creamy froth of the milk he had delivered every morning before he had come to be in this crazy situation. The milk he had to escape from, a confrontation with his father being the first time he'd stood up for himself. So here he was on another milkrun, the name base gave these missions, but this time delivering bombs to the kitchens of Remscheid.

Back then he'd told his father he wasn't going to work on that darned dairy farm any more. Didn't everyone know there was a war on? The Prime Minister had made a call on the radio for volunteers. And he had already volunteered, so there was nothing anyone could do. He had put his name down for the Empire Air Training Scheme, and signed himself into the Air Cadet Corps that was training boys for the Royal Australian Air Force. He had been assigned night duty on the roof of the Town Hall on the look-out for Japanese planes, and artillery practice was promised too, as soon as the guns were available for it.

But his father had heard other Prime Ministers and other waist-coated men give pompous speeches on honour and duty and sacrifice. Mr Piggott had a wife and five children, and he had honours and duties and sacrifices of his own. The swagger and drama of an air force life, travelling to Europe, flying Tiger Moths or Ansons or Oxfords, or some of the newer, bigger bombers that were rumoured to be flying in England, was lost on him. He saw only the lack of another pair of hands. Life for a dairyman-vendor was an aching routine relieved only by the variations in the seasons. No matter whether there was ice on the ground, or the sun blazed down on drought parched paddocks, the milking still needed to be done. And after that the milk had to be delivered, the horse drawing the cart and a sweating Piggott running from cart to house all over Maitland. The delivery had to be rushed so that the horses were off the road before the rest of the world got moving in cars and lorries. It wasn't a life which permitted much consideration of anything other than the waxing and waning output of the udders of a herd of Jerseys. Each drop of the white fluid represented more money for the family business. The more hands there were to work the warm, wrinkled teats on those udders, the better the return for the family. And even in the best times, that return was very meagre.

"I'm in. It's official," Neil had told his father. It was not quite true. As he was under age, his father's formal permission was still required. Surprisingly, his father had said nothing and put his signature on the form without reading it. He kept silent his concerns about how he and Harry would cope with the milking, the hand turning of the separator which lifted the cream from the milk, and the laborious washing of the machines. And there was no mention of the stop and start drive through the sleeping town, a quiet pilgrimage from house to house filling billies or whatever suitable container had been put out in readiness for the frothy milk. The Piggotts had acquired a special status in Maitland, not just because they brought milk to every house, but also because they were trusted to enter unlit kitchens in the secret morning hours. The boys had been taught from a very early age to remain silent about whatever might be seen in that spectral light. So the Piggotts were burdened with a good number of closed door truths, which did them no harm when it came to the weekly payments, or gifts at Christmas. And the white, fatty fluid they brought to the town was regarded as essential. So essential that dairy farmers were exempt from compulsory military service.

So why, reasoned Neil's father, would Neil want to leave the family now, to go off to foreign countries, dirty and full of poverty, the lot of them, where death was not a likelihood but a certainty, and leaving so much extra work to fall on the shoulders of those whom he had left behind? His mother and sisters, as well, would be forced to carry extra loads. The fresh field mushrooms and eggs the family offered in addition to the milk and cream it supplied the townsfolk would have to be gathered and prepared by someone, if Neil wasn't there to do it. It seemed a selfish and stupid thing for him to do, especially without discussing it first. Anyway, it was pretty clear from the papers that it'd be over soon anyway so what was the use. Yet Mr Piggott stayed silent on all of this. He had listened to Neil, and taken in his son's desperate urge to find a wider world.

Neil had expected his father to argue further. But the dairy farmer didn't. He might not have believed the words Neil was uttering, but they had behind them all the strength and threats of officialdom. The name of the King had been invoked many times before in his life in order to separate him from something he had thought his. And Neil had clearly passed the point where the dictates of parental control were observed. Mr Piggott would make no further comment with regard to the burden Neil was placing on the family. He could see his son had made up his mind, and he was of an age where that had to be respected, no matter what the consequences.

There was no use trying to talk him out of it, Neil had said. He was a patriot, he told his father, he was going to fight for his King and country. The recruiting posters and the leaflets from the Government had words saying similar things printed on them. Neil mouthed them without conviction for he had only vague feelings about Australia, and was sure of only one thing about the King, George VI, and that was it was his head which was called on when a coin was tossed in the air for a bet. He knew these empty words did not spell out the reason why he wanted to join the Air Force. He knew that it was boredom which drove him, boredom with the confining regularity of life in his little town. Boredom with having lived seventeen years all exactly like the one before. And war, portrayed in the lofty words and sanitised pictures of army bureaucracy, promised an escape.

When the time came for Neil to leave, his father drove him to the railway station in the familiar old milk wagon. He'd waited with Neil on the platform until the train had pulled in, wraiths of steam hissing from it, then he'd taken Neil's hand and said: "Don't be an idiot and get in the way of the guns, will you son. A dozen or more of my mates are buried over in France because they got in the way of the guns in that last war. Lot of people call them heroes. I reckon all of them would rather be called alive."

Once he'd found his seat Neil had looked out onto the platform to wave goodbye to his father, but the dairy farmer had already left, enough precious time lost from the regularity of his unchanging day. When Neil returned, years later, his father had welcomed him back with an outstretched hand. "Good to have you back, son," was all he said, then he left for the milking shed. Though when the family was shown the medal, after a week or more of constant pleading from his sisters and Harry and Harry's new wife, Neil heard his father whisper: "I thought they only gave dead men this". Which was about the time Neil was beginning to wonder if, indeed, that was what they had done.

Then there was England and a girl, Bernice, he had come to know at the pub in the village near the base. She had white, smooth thighs between her suspenders and the tops of her stockings. He'd touched those thighs the night before. He'd kissed her goodnight at the end of the lane that led to her house. It was dark, all lights blacked out, so no-one had seen his hands slide up under her skirt. She'd shivered at his touch, but not told him to stop. "Come back safely," she'd told him, "and we can do this again."

"Watch out for the coast," he called to the navigator. "Once we're over the water we'll radio base to let them know we're coming in with a few cuts and bruises." They were somewhere over Holland now. "Jack, can you get a fix? Where are we?" Jack read back co-ordinates, and Neil altered course. There was not much moon but the light of what there was on the sea would help orientate them a little more, and he could fly lower. He spoke into the intercom: "Dusty, how's the weather back there?"

A laboured voice replied: "Not too good Skip. I've taken something in my left leg."

"How bad?"

"I'm bleeding buckets." And he'd kept silent. Dusty was a constant surprise. Neil quickly checked the rest of the crew. Mac the mid-upper gunner was dead. Mercifully, the first round had taken him so he hadn't felt the flames burning around him. Then he took reports on the plane's condition. The astrodome had been shot off, the flaps were damaged but only a landing would show how bad, the hydraulics were out and he had only two engines. The good news was they were still flying, and appeared to have lost the fighter on their tail. Life could be worse, he thought. But the memory of Bernice's thighs told him it could be better, too. She would go with him, and they'd find a warm space somewhere to lie down in. He'd kiss her, and she'd kiss him. And he'd go under her dress and touch her thighs, undo her suspenders, roll down her stockings . . .

"Skip, Dusty's bad." Bill had managed to work his way down the plane to Dusty's lonely pod in the rear. "But I've given him oxygen."

"Still bleeding?"

"Yes, Skip. I've done what I can to staunch it, but his leg's all smashed."

"We're over the coast," Bill noted.

"Tim?" Neil called to his radio operator, "call up base and get them to clear an airfield for us. We're going to have to come in belly-up."

Bill clambered back into position. Jack, the bomb aimer, had crawled past him to be down in the tail beside Dusty.

"Take her Bill. I'm going back to see Dusty," Neil said. He released his harness and clambered to his feet. Turning round, he caught a look of disgust from Tim, whose boots were sloshing in half-frozen piss.

"This is no way to fly, Skipper," Tim said as Neil squeezed past him and felt his way down the gloomy fuselage. This was no way to do anything, Neil thought, but there was no boredom in it. The acrid fumes of the fire, the icy air blasting at him through whistling holes in the fuselage, the sickening lurches of the stricken plane that left him clutching whatever solid shape was nearest, these were all immeasurably more enlivening than the twice daily peregrinations of cud-chewing cows.

If he'd been at home, he'd have been asleep now. Though fitfully. The cows ambling in bovine mindlessness up the still dark paddocks, their instinctive forms pushing through the ground mist, the wet pasture, driven towards the milking shed by the pressure in their udders. Those massive shadows would rustle their bulk through his sleep, a nightmare of reality which in the end propelled him into wakefulness. Into his milking clothes, waiting at the end of the bed. The gumboots, outside near the back door on the verandah. Lighting the kerosene lamp for the downhill trek to the milking shed. And then, in the lamp's pool of light, into the paddocks, Kippie charging through the grass ahead, eager for the smells and scents come new with the night, ready to get behind and nip the slowest of the herd straggling towards the dim light his father and brother were working to in the shed.

His father and older brother Harry would work, each on a stool, hands under beasts in the slips, squeezing, squeezing, squeezing. The twice daily torture of the dairy farmer. Seventeen, he'd been milking all his life. His fingers even in sleep would shape for the squeeze. Teats — soft, yielding, spurting teats. Teats surprisingly clean and soft and warm, but still needing a wipe before the squeezing could begin. Teats with mastitis, still needing to be milked but the milk useless. He saw his bare hands reaching to grip an udder to squeeze for milk.

The cows themselves. Big, brown eyes, sensuous pools to fall in love in, but the animals stupid. All day munching grass. With all day and night to empty themselves before milking. Yet at least one would let loose a stream of sloppy, green shit just as a bucket had filled. Or burp fermenting grass into a face not yet fully awake. Another, after years of quietly observing the monotonous daily routine, would suddenly find a reason to panic. At what only her small mind could know. But a cow trying to leap out of the race, eyes popping, nostrils flaring, at least relieved the back-breaking tedium of teat squeezing, even if a lot of milk ended up spilt. And that milk. Thick with cream. Warm. Foaming with bubbles.

He hated the milk. He wouldn't drink it, not by itself, not in tea or coffee, not as cocoa. In the mess others would down glasses of cold milk when it was available. Most of the men were from the city, dull suburbs of two-up, two-down terraces, toilets out the back with the sanitary collector more familiar than a milkman. Little enough money for bread, and that stale from the corner shop. Milk practically a luxury. He'd let them have his. Milk was for the cat. The big ratter which stalked the milking shed. In early morning, he'd see its eyes reflecting the lamp's flame as it lurked in the dark, waiting for the milking to begin. Then it would saunter nearer, circling, advancing, retreating, the smell of the milk pulling it closer and closer to the light and the bustle in the shed. Harry and Neil would wait till she had twitched herself within range, then one of them would hit her with a stream of milk. It was what the cat was waiting for. Sometimes she would leap up, or stretch on her hind legs, to catch as much of the stream in her mouth as she could. Other times she would let herself be hit by the jet of warm, white liquid, then spend ecstatic minutes licking it from her fur.

The cat provided almost the only break they had from the tedium. Seven days a week, three hundred and sixty five days a year, they had to be up before dawn for milking, and again in the afternoon. When he'd gone to school, he'd do the milking then pedal his old bike the fifteen dusty miles to the one teacher school at Fingal's Creek. In summer, he'd leave earlier to avoid the heat, but no matter what the season he'd pedal in bare feet. There was no money for shoes other than gumboots, and you couldn't wear them to school. He didn't think about being barefoot much, because most of the other kids at the school were as well. But, when he'd volunteered, been passed as medically fit, and was being measured for his uniform, his feet had been too broad for the usual boot. The air force had had to have some specially made for him. He'd worn the best pair they could come up with for the two weeks it took for his to be made. He'd been almost crippled with blisters and cramps.

Then the long hours of learning to fly. There was routine in that, the repeated take-offs and landings, the drills, the checklists. But each day brought something a little different. It might be cockpit drill, and then straight and level flight. Or cockpit drill and stalls. Medium turns. Taking off into wind. Gliding. Instrument flying. Powered approach and landing. His hands squeezed the stick of the DH 82 he trained on much like he squeezed udders. The response from the little plane was entirely different, giving him the chance to soar up and away from the bovine monotony of dairy-farming. If he could fly, he could do anything. Life was suddenly full of options.

Until he arrived in Europe. The option was Bernice, and he was not sure she'd be willing to go all the way. He'd take precautions, of course. He wasn't sure he wanted to marry her, and he didn't want to be forced to. But she was reason enough, now.

Her, alone, just for the lust of it. And Dusty, whom he would return for burial in a place more friendly than occupied Europe. Already Dusty's boots were full of blood and the shock had made him rigid. Jack and Neil wrapped the injured man with any extra coverings they could dredge from the plane's few hiding places. They made him as comfortable as a seat on a parachute would permit.

"You've got to stay awake Dusty," Neil told him, "or you'll miss breakfast."

After a mission, the mess laid on a breakfast of crisp rashers, potatoes, kidneys, fresh toast and coffee. Then the crews would meander off base to become thoroughly whistled; totally, utterly wasted. Though Dusty wouldn't be with them this time.

Neil shuffled his way back up front and took the controls again. "About half an hour to base," Tim's voice came through the intercom. "They're standing by."

"Good-oh," he replied. The flight was back under control, now, order restored.

Yet he was thinking of flames. He was still hearing the screams through the intercom. He was searching the sky for the flares that would tell him he had a field he could ditch in.

The plane was steadily dropping. Lower and lower. There was only enough fuel for six minutes more flying. Then he'd have no choice at all. He knew he had no ailerons. As well, the undercarriage was unresponsive to hydraulic or manual commands. The mechanics had been shot to pieces by that damned Me109, so it was going to have to be a belly landing. But more chance where there was an airfield with fire trucks and groundcrew, provided they could make it. No chance otherwise.

"Skipper, any sign of anything," his navigator screamed through the intercom.

He didn't bother to answer. It would take too much precious time. The flight engineer gave him a thumbs up. Neil didn't know what for. Bill had been working wonders with his toolkit and had managed to patch some of the damage. The plane was responding a little more gracefully to its pilot. But they were still a long way from base.

He heard: "His boots are full of blood. I don't reckon he's going to make it."

Dusty was fading. The blood was still flowing out of him. They were going to crash. There was no hope left.

No, Neil don't think like that. Keep your hands steady on the stick. Keep the old bird up as long as you can. Any minute you will see a flare. Any minute.

And there it is. Now the whole field flickering on for them, twin lines of beautiful, welcoming lights. He has to work it like the book. Cut power. Come in gliding. He can use the tail for direction, but he can't do much to control his speed. He's going to come in much too fast. Hold the nose up, hold it up for as long as possible. Bang! They are down and skidding across the field, sparks shooting up all around them. Slowing, slowing, screeching to a standstill. He rips open his harness and pelts for the hatch. It is already open. The rest of the crew are helping each other out, struggling with Dusty. Neil goes back down the plane to drag the body of the mid-upper gunner to the hatch where now the ground crew are reaching in to assist.

He drops out onto the ground and staggers away from the wreck.

I'm alive, he thinks, I'm bloody alive.

"Skipper," Bill came up to him. "Skipper, you beauty! You saved us all. They've got to give you a medal for that."

I'm bloody alive. Fear, late and uncalled, suddenly flooded him, and he gagged and vomited. He had returned most of his crew alive, destroyed his plane, and survived a flight which great numbers of his squadron had not. But he didn't know that yet, or why on such occasions heroes became necessary. That was one thing he would never understand. In a secret place inside him, a male form that had his name was curling itself into a ball, shutting its eyes tightly, and covering its ears with its hands.

Then he and the rest of the crew climbed aboard a lorry to go to the mess and eat.

That night, with a few whiskies in him, Neil asked Bernice if she remembered what they had talked about a previous night, and her promise. She smiled at him. "Would you like to go for a walk, Flight-Sergeant?" she asked.

He remembered her kindness years later when his grandson Kieran came out of the dark on another night at Mt Kuring-gai to ask for his grandfather's help. The boy arrived about nine-thirty. He had a backpack and suitcase. He came through the kitchen door where Eileen was putting away warm plates and cutlery fresh from the dishwasher. Neil was up in the TV room.

"Is my grand-dad here?" he asked. "I've got to see him."

"You poor thing," she said, "whatever's happened. Sit down and I'll get you something."

"Please. Can I see Neil?"

Neil came out to hear what all the noise was.

"Kieran! What's wrong? What are you doing here at this time of night?"

Kieran burst into tears.

"Hey!" His grandfather moved over to put his arm around the boy's shoulders. "Let's go for a walk and you can tell me what's up."

The two of them strolled out down the drive and around the block. When they returned half an hour later, Kieran was no longer crying. Eileen had made up a bed for him, which he went straight to, and slept the sleep of the innocent.

In the morning, the conversation Kieran had had with his grandfather was one more secret for Neil to hold onto. In the long years since he had been singed in the furnace of war, Neil had maintained the silence the unspeakable secrets in his mind required. He had been awarded for the work he had done to save his aircrew, and as a consequence was ranked as one of his country's greatest heroes. He had accepted his medal, and the noble words that accompanied it, because it was his duty to do so. In his mind, though, he knew he was not braver or better than any of the men with whom he had served. And he could not reconcile his high honour with the fact that he had survived, whilst many of those with whom he had served had died. This was his secret, the secret of the brave soldier forced to play the hero, but so very, very unwilling to accept the part.

Neil knew secrets: the tortuous pain of their insight and the continuous sting of their pretence. So he could listen to Kieran, and understand.

And Neil was warmed to know that this last secret at least was shared with his wife and grandson.

Thursday, January 14, 1993
Mt Kuring-gai, Australia
5:49 a.m.

His erection wakes him, a dull ache in the wet heat of a Sydney summer morning. He has just a sheet over him, but sweat still sticks it to him. It presses down on him, lightly, moistly, as she had done.

She had offered Alex her breasts, her hands cupped underneath them. She moved her body forward so her right nipple touched his lips. She stroked it across, then around.

His tongue slipped out, unbidden, and lapped round. First the nipple then more of the milky white breast. He noticed the veins, a pinky-blue tracing of support under the skin. Her breasts were mildly coloured, like almost all of her. But down below there was the change in skin colour where the small satin white sea of flesh profiled her black map of Tasmania.

A strand of her red hair fell down. He brushed it away to keep it out of his mouth. The left breast pushed at his face. Her CD player sighed a plaintive North African wail. The chant, the insistent rhythm, the high-pitched pipes, rolled into his ears, slipped deep inside, and turned inside out to become the animal growling in him. His whole body was being taken over, all muscles and sinew, claws and teeth.

It was then Alyson had leaned right over to take his right nipple between her teeth and bite.

"Shit!" The sudden nip, the jolt through his body, flashed passages of his brother's diary before him. His brother had recounted tales of sharper, more intense sexuality. Alex did not want those scenes played out here, with Alyson.

"You don't like it?" she'd hissed, teeth still holding the little nipple, his breath faster, body tensed further.

"It hurts."

"But do you like it?" Her warm breath close heat on his body, a soothing pleasure supplementing the intense one her teeth were providing. Drums and flutes reached a small climax in the music.

"Yes," he had sighed. Her teeth slowly let go. He could now feel everything, even the delicate touch of his own long lashes brushing the bones of his cheeks. Was this how his brother had felt, he had wondered, this letting go? And he could feel that no matter who it was with, the degree of sensation was irresistible. The tight, percussive secrets of his body; rapid descants and sudden pizzicatos, his own wild improvisation first slowly snaking out the notes, then pulsing in strong, confident tones.

His body was released; his rational self, his mind, had melted out into the very outermost layers of his skin, where it frizzled and jolted the electricity of pure sensation all over him. Her fingers, her breasts, the scent of her; her half-closed eyes as she moved herself upon him; the music, hypnotic, insistent, strange yet increasingly familiar; all had worked their magic. The beast had broken through the thin veneer on the surface. His body was all panting, tingling intensity. His tongue lolled out to lick her breast, which on that day was filmed with the oil of her heat. The touch and taste of her a giddy swoon. He brought his teeth closed on her nipple, too, and she laughed.

"Yes, yes, but not too hard," she had said. And he could see his brother in an orgy with other men, and he could understand the different pleasure.

He recalls that later she had been straddling his stomach. Her pubic hair, which he remembers as being so surprisingly black and bushy when the hair on her head was so red, had brushed his skin into goosebumps when she had first climbed onto him. He felt her wetness seeping, then drying on his skin, above the cord of his swimmers. He had left them on. He didn't know when he should take them off. He'd never done this with anyone else. Only with himself, imagining what it might be like, which was nothing like the tickling thrill of her skin against his. Her breath on his bellybutton. His cock was so hard. He shook with the effort of willing it not to shoot. Though drops of clear fluid oozed through from the tip as it moistened in readiness. She'll see, he'd thought. Her face was centimetres from it. Then she moved her leg across his head and pushed her own wetness onto his mouth. And he lapped into her.

Her tongue traced a snail's track down the shape in his swimmers. She licked again, from the top down to his balls. Very, very gently, but he twitched and shook with the ecstasy of it.

She moved up. Sitting above his face. His own tongue was wriggling into the spaces it was finding before it. His hands reached up and opened her a little more. He let the joy of the darkness take him.

Then she had moved around, her body down, so she was kneeling astride his swimmers and the warm wetness was seeping through. He thought he was going to come right then, but she moved with infinite slowness, waiting for his breathing to ease. She kissed his wet lips, her tongue bringing their flavours together. A passing cloud let sunlight expand across their bodies. The salty smell of her was rich in his nostrils.

She had begun to undo the string that held his speedos, and to slip them down to his thighs. He was suddenly conscious of his ribs, too prominent, making him appear exceptionally thin.

His eyes spring open. His vision of her fades. Instead of her opulent flesh he sees his brother Kieran's body, drooping like a sunflower does as it fades, with that same mouldy odour of decay. He can see the flannelette dressing gown falling off shoulders too frail to hold it up. Kieran's eyes too large in his shrunken head, distorted out of shape by the growths in his left jaw and under his chin.

Get out of my mind, he tells this memory. I want to remember her again, not you, not now.

He stares at the ceiling, willing her warm skin, her breasts, her mango of a mound to come back and replay that sensuous afternoon when he had slipped and slid into condoms and ultimately into her. But she will not reappear.

"Self-control," he whispers. The words are just more liquid in the predawn summer humidity.

He lies in a room in his grandfather's house, that glorious afternoon refusing to surface again on his sea of remembrance. I was learning self-control, he tells himself. But he wants to remember the pleasure more intensely. His cock is ready for it, jutting up against the sheet, his right hand close by. He holds back. It would be a momentary spurt of pleasure.

No exhilarated togetherness such as he'd shared with Alyson Ford, even though she'd turned on him. Used him. Told him she had done it. "You were an available boy," she had said, "and I needed you. But once will do both of us nicely thanks." He'd felt bad about that, at first. But after a day or so, he was revelling in the sensuous freedom of it. And right now he would love to be used in just that way, again and again.

He knows he has been lucky for a seventeen year old. There'll be many more times, he's sure, now he knows what a woman likes. He had been timid, but she had dragged him out of his metaphorical corner, and let the uncivilised part of him come alive on her bed. And in the bathroom. And against the wall. An afternoon where he had come time after time, his young stamina a toy in her experienced hands. Before, he had never thought of being with an older woman like Alyson, a woman able to guide and not afraid to say, and do. It has been only girls his own age whom he's thought about before. And magazine pictures. Nothing like the voluptuous flesh that lay itself upon him and slipped him inside. He wants to feel that release again, but he closes his fingers so that they will not provide the slippery caress.

His brother comes back in a noisy rush. The wheeze of his lungs rattling with the fight for air.

Pain and joy all a forest of confusion, like her bush that had smelt of the sea and into which his face pushed. His eyes blinded by her thighs and his mouth eager for the warm, wet taste of her.

It had all started on the next day, the one after the funeral, a week ago. Alyson Ford had suddenly, stridently been on the phone again. Only this time she was ringing to speak with Alex. Everything about it was unusual, even at that unusual time, and Alex was wary from the beginning. Alyson up until then had been the loud counsellor who kept the keys to his dying brother's world. Alex was merely a small satellite set into orbit around that particular universe. He sensed there was more to her words than what she actually said.

"You're probably feeling rotten", she had said, "which is only natural. Why don't you come out with me and I'll try to cheer you up?" He was feeling extremely miserable, but so too were his grandfather Neil and Eileen, his step-grandmother. The three of them had been gently soothing each other since the ceremony. Since Alyson had had more to do with Neil, Alex wondered why he was being singled out.

"Out where?" he asked.

"Maybe the beach. Maybe to a movie. Anything."

"Why?"

"Are you having heaps of fun up there? I'm not down here, and I've got the day off, so if I don't do something I'll just get myself drunk. It's a hazard in my job. Trying to find a means to ease the stress. So I thought maybe the two of us could help each other. You could keep me on the straight and narrow and I can, well, I can do something to make you feel better." Though surrounded by the quiet of Mt Kuring-gai, and in a house gloomed with the death of his brother, Alex was not entirely unattuned to an invitation which promised some fun, and perhaps a little more. He was still seventeen. He had planned nothing for the day, expecting that he would wake up in a funereal mood, which he had. In the hours before Alyson had rung Neil, Eileen and he had had a sad breakfast. Then, Alex had fed the magpies, watered the back garden and started listening to a CD on his Discman. Neil had made himself busy in his workshed, his electric saw irregularly whining a metallic dirge into a sky washed blue by the rain of the day before. Eileen had set about baking Anzac biscuits, which she had been doing on every Thursday every week for more years than she cared to remember.

"It'll take me ages to get there. I'll have to change trains at Hornsby," he told her.

"Tell you what. I'll meet you in the City. On the Town Hall steps at 11.30. That'll give you plenty of time. Do you want to go out to Coogee for a swim?"

Which is what they did. He had hurried to the station to wait impatiently for a slow train. He now had an anticipation, fuelled by the unexpectedness of the invitation and a mischievous tone in Alyson's voice. He had thought he was ready for her from the very first. He had easily responded to her first calculated move, though he had not always known what was expected of him.

She had packed a picnic into her backpack. Boiled eggs, cabanossi, artichokes, fresh Turkish bread, cheese, mangoes, and baklava. She had him wear the pack. It was a sleek black leather bag, with stainless steel buckles and rivets, very smart in design. She'd had it made for her in Turkey. The straps around his shoulder pulled his tee-shirt tight against his body, and Alyson noted the sinewy thinness of it, supple with youth, though gangly still at the elbows and knees as the last of his childhood grew out of him. He wore a jacket tied by the sleeves around his waist, long baggy shorts, oversized baseball shoes and a goofy hat she wanted to tear off his head. But he had made an effort for her, wearing what his peers had defined as the latest look.

She was wearing shorts, too, but briefer and tighter than his. There was more of her than there was of him. She had put on a loose, floppy top with long sleeves for protection against the sun. Her hat was a wide-brimmed Akubra, and her sunglasses were recommended by the Cancer Foundation. She'd picked up her sandals in Thailand at a little market on Koh Samui. They were purple and black, matching her top. He asked her about them, as he couldn't help noticing them. But he did not say whether or not he liked them.

At the end of the bus route, they stepped out of the bus with a few others then dawdled across the landscaped beachfront onto the beach. There were not too many people there. A few tourists, and a smattering of locals still on their Christmas break. But the bulk of Sydney had departed north or south, where the coast was now a blanket of flesh; thousands of mothers and fathers and children lying in a wash of sunscreen and 34 degree heat, alone with each other on holiday.

The two of them were able to settle on a clear patch of sand not far from the flags. They spread out towels and a small cloth, and set up lunch.

"Can you go over the road and get some drinks?" she had asked. He crossed over to the shops and bought two cans of ginger beer. When he came back, she had him take off his shirt and shorts, and she rubbed sunscreen over him. It was easy to add a few playful strokes to this ritual. Rubbing up his thighs towards his swimmers, and on his stomach and back. He said nothing, but she could feel the tightness of his interest.

"Your turn to do me," she said, and pulled her top off over her head. She smiled at him, and his staring at her breasts.

"Start up here," she said, "I don't want my tits burned off." He rubbed the cream into her all over, his movements strong and dedicated, with no sensuousness at all. But he knew he was being seduced, and he was enjoying the game.

Once they were duly protected, hats and sunglasses back on as well, they started to eat. Some of the food was unfamiliar to him, but she made him try it all, even if only a little bit.

It was one of those summer days when Sydney decides to be perfect. Heaven could have been only a Chocolate Heart away. The air was full of the sea, rather than the smell of traffic. The sky was southern blue; the only blue. The water was unusually clear and clean. There was a swell, a small rip, and many people were bodysurfing. The two of them sat in silence watching the surfers and swimmers, letting their food settle. Then he wanted to feel the water on him, stretch himself through it, let its coolness kiss away the heat.

"I'm going to have a swim," he said.

"I think I will too."

"Yeah? I was going to try and catch a few waves."

"You don't mind if we do it together?"

"Nah. Course not." He might have realised what she was doing, but once she began to fully exercise her skills he found he was in a foreign place, and he didn't know the language. He was just what she wanted then, he was the toy she'd decided to play with.

They had gone out into the water together. They found a spot where they could catch the swell, and not be near other swimmers. He was watching the sea more carefully than her and caught the first one. Alyson watched him be carried in the foam almost to the shore. He stood up and ran back through the water towards her, a sea-washed smile transforming his gawky run through the knee-deep water into ineffable elegance. He looked now so much like his brother had when she had first met him. It was her job that was driving her crazy. She was counselling only for friends and family of the terminally ill. She had to smile every working moment, and there was every reason not to.

They both caught the next wave. This one had a curve in it that dumped Alex on top of her. She took a mouthful of water, then, as she pushed him off her, grabbed his head and ducked him. It was a quick, unexpected action, and he had no resistance. Then the boy in him reacted. He took a mouthful of water and spat it at her face.

"You filthy little pig!" She splashed a fistful of water at him. He was laughing. She saw her moment. She grabbed him, and reached down for a handful of wet sand. She thrust it quickly down the back of his speedos.

"That'll learn you," she shouted back to him as she arched away to safety in deeper water. He had to swim out far enough to where he could loosen his swimmers so the sand would wash out. He was learning a foreign language fast. The cool water chilled his excitement away.

Then he swam out to where she was lazily floating on her back, eye out for a suitable wave. Her breasts intrigued him. They changed shape as her body changed position. The big, brown nipples had softened and flattened now she was in the water. He dived down to the bottom and scooped up sand in his hands. He kicked himself straight up to the surface and he dumped the sand in a glorious splat over her breasts.

She spluttered upright, and lunged at him. He put up his hands to fend her off, and her breasts came smacking into them. And his hands were reaching around her. Her hand was on the back of his head, guiding it towards her mouth. His mouth towards her mouth. He embraced her fully as their lips met.

Later, after a laughing taxi ride to Leichhardt, he was marvelling again at how, as she lay naked on her back on the bed, her breasts spread out, almost disappeared. Their shape faded into her chest with only the darkness of the nipple showing. Between her legs, he could see the smoothed and saturated edges of that black, black hair. He knew, too, though he couldn't see it from the other side of the room where he sat in a chair sipping coffee, that a thin line of the black hair traced its way up to her navel.

It was after. She had him make the coffee. She wouldn't allow him to get back on the bed with her. She needed a bit of space, she said. She hadn't touched her coffee, which was growing cold on the bedside table.

"Kieran wasn't circumcised. How come you are? Brothers are usually the same," she said finally.

"What do you mean?" he asked. He was reliving every contour of her body. His brother was another landscape. "You did this with him as well?"

"No. But I saw him being washed, Alex. I undressed him and helped him into bed. I didn't do this with him. This is just for you and me, to help us get over him." To help me, she thought, get over all of them. She was going to have to resign soon.

"Would you have wanted to do it with him, then? Even knowing he was a poof?"

She paused, very slightly.

"I wanted to do it with him ever since I first saw him. He was what I wanted all my life. Handsome, athletic, intelligent. Yeah, a real spunk." She had also wanted to do it with the shaven headed bikie with the tattooed biceps who lived across the road and had a dumb blonde girlfriend. And with the Maori bodybuilder who shopped at the health food store on Saturday mornings, and who had winked at her once. And with the businessman carrying the briefcase who walked his daughter to school past the newsagent where she bought the paper every morning. And with at least five men every day, just passing, or reflected in a window, or walking. But she'd picked seventeen year old Alex instead.

"So I'm just a surrogate for that. You really wanted him, but you ended up with me."

A long sigh. A burp. A double vodka suggested itself, and unconsciousness.

"No mate, don't lose your shirt. There were heaps of boys I wanted. There are heaps of boys I want. I like all sorts of boys. I love different types of guys. I would really like to be a big slut and just have different men around all the time, get off on it. But the ones I end up feeling really deeply for, the ones who get me all hung up, they inevitably turn out to be gay guys. I like men, Alex, but for reasons I don't understand and wish I did I like gay men best, only they don't like me like I like men. That's the big pain in my life. I'm sorry, I didn't mean to draw you into all this. I like you."

"You think I'm gay and that's why you slept with me?" His sensitivity was a blunt instrument.

"No, mate. No, I don't think you're gay at all, and that's why I slept with you. Because I couldn't sleep with your brother, I couldn't sleep with any of them. I tried to, all the time, but none of them wanted me."

"So I was an easy target. You could have me, easy." He could feel her mood growing into a dark shape filling the space between her and him.

She turned and smiled at him: "Yeah. You got a problem with that? I didn't think you did a few minutes ago. You seemed to enjoy what we did."

"I did. Why are you spoiling it?" He had been so alive and electric, and now he ached.

"I can't help myself I guess. I'm an idiot." She wanted him to leave. She didn't want to have a relationship with him, just a fuck. He couldn't like her. She was too old and ugly. He should just leave whistling, glad to have got his rocks off.

"What do you mean by that?"

"I shouldn't have dragged you into this. I'm just such a mess. Like, I'm at the clinic most days, or at people's homes checking they're o.k. I'm chasing all these guys, right, who I really like. They're all nice blokes. I get really close to them. Then they die. What am I saying this to you for? I've been a total fuckwit. I'm so sorry Alex. Today was a day when I could relax and do just what I wanted. I've used you. I thought, 'how can I have sex with no complications' and you came to mind. "An available young man', I thought, 'who won't say no to an afternoon romp'. And I was right wasn't I? But, Alex, though I might have used you, you have been really good for me. I needed the time we spent today. You probably think I'm a total madwoman by now. I don't blame you. Maybe you'll think better of me later."

"What are you on about? If you used me, I wanted it that way. It was great. I was basically a virgin, Alyson. I guess you could tell. But I didn't want to be. I thought we were having fun. Isn't that what you wanted? Did I do something wrong?" He tried, with his limited knowledge of the realm they had entered, to negotiate her back to him.

"Not at all. In fact, you saved me." She was sober, and it was late afternoon.

"What do you mean?"

"Most days I have off I start with a double vodka. That's breakfast. I keep going on the bottle, take some pills, black out. I know it's a stupid thing to do and that it's killing me, but it's how I cope. Only today I tried a different method. Here I am in the afternoon sober and clear-headed, just a little guilty about dragging you into my sordid universe. But you liked it, didn't you?"

"You didn't?"

"Yeah, Alex. It was fine. No, it was more than that. It was really good. I had a good orgasm. Women don't always, you know. But I was on top. That helped."

"Yeah, that was good."

"I was directing things how I like them. You know, maybe there's a moral for me there. I know I'm suffering burnout, but if I can get on top of things, I'll be getting back in control."

"You want to get on top of me, again? Can we do it again then?" He tried to use her directness against her, but she was seventeen years ahead of him.

"You cheeky kid! 'Almost a virgin', and now you want to party all day long. No. That's the end. We've just done it as a ceremony, a way of mourning Kieran. And all the others. I'm so sick of my job, Alex. I've got to have some life, like this, or write myself off. Or I'll go crazy. I didn't mean to do you any harm, mate, but this is just a one off. I don't want to do it again."

"Yeah. I was kind of expecting that."

"Of course, I could hire you. Bring you over on my days off and pay you to be my little sex toy."

"But I'd just be a prostitute!"

"A gigolo, actually. Doesn't turn you on?"

"How much would you pay me?"

She had thrown her head back snorting with laughter. When she calmed down, she gave him a kiss, affectionate and gentle.

"I am going to miss your brother," she had said. "But I'll know you'll still be around. Tell me, I was curious that you're circumcised, yet Kieran wasn't. Usually it runs the same way in a family."

"I dunno. I don't know anything about that. My parents did it. My foreskin had a problem when I was little. Something like that. But I don't want to talk about my brother's cock."

She had unerringly found the place where she could distance him from her.

In the sticky heat of his bed, he runs his left index finger over his right nipple; his body throbs with the pleasure. The finger moves one by one over his ribs, then down a curve over his diaphragm, and some ridged muscles of his stomach. He's pleased by them, they have much more shape and definition this way than when seen in the mirror. He doesn't like his body when he looks at it. But touch is different. His navel is a slight hollow. Tight muscles below down to the brown groin hairs. He remembers the scent of her breast; and the flesh of it pressing into his face.

He will not let his right hand do what it wants to do.

He's already covered with a thin layer of sweat as the heat of the January day explodes. This summer there have been few days which haven't dawned cleanly blue, with the steam already rising. It is drought time. The dry is so bad there has been talk that even Sydney will have its water rationed. There have been bushfire scares, too. These have worried Neil and Eileen, who have pruned their garden away from the house. Now they are obsessed with keeping every plant green. Since he came here before Christmas he's been out nearly every morning with his grandfather toting buckets of water to the lemon trees, the prized roses, or worst of all the vegetable garden, which is arm-numbingly right up the back of the yard. Yet the weather remains insufferably humid, each little movement producing streams of sweat.

Before Christmas, there had been some desultory showers. More lightning and thunder than rain. But that had been another time, like a dream now. The HSC had finished. He was suddenly cut off from school. An absence of routine left him sleepless. He was up early and home late. He'd gone to friends' houses to have parties, to the beach to swim and sunbake. At night he'd been going to movies, to see bands play if the bouncers didn't ask for ID, and eaten endless pizzas and hamburger meals, free at last just to have fun.

He had been making plans to go up to Byron Bay. Thommo and Vlad were going up there. Thommo's parents had a flat, suddenly and unseasonably with no tenant. The three of them were going to drive up in Vlad's car. They had worked out they'd share petrol, pay a bit for the flat to compensate for lost rent, and see what they had left to divide between food and whatever seemed like a good idea at the time.

But he'd forgotten to take the joint out of his shirt pocket.

"No way," his father said, "no way are you going anywhere there's no adult supervision."

"I can't believe it," his mother said, "after all the things we've told you about drugs. This is just too much. Especially after all we've been through this year. I'm very disappointed in you Alex."

So Alex was forbidden to go. Even though he was seventeen. Even though Vlad had tried to convince Alex's father he would keep Alex out of trouble: "I'll make sure he's in bed by ten every night. Honest. He won't get into strife, believe me. We're going to do everything by the book. Three meals a day. Lots of swimming and exercise. No alcohol. No smoking. And we'll be real careful driving, Mr Piggott, the car can't go too fast anyway." And Thommo had said, "It's a real nice flat, nothing scungy or anything. It's right near the beach at Wattego's." Vlad and Thommo didn't think the joint was anything to get too excited about, and neither did Alex. Everybody smoked. Thommo's parents smoked, even in front of Thommo. Alex thought even his parents might once have taken a puff. His father had all those old seventies records by Cream and Iron Butterfly and Spooky Tooth with the over-the-top drug references. And his father had had hippie hair and a beard when he'd gone to university. But now his father had become a born again health vigilante Alex had found his own freedom more and more circumscribed. Being denied a trip to Byron Bay was definitely the worst that had happened, though. The cruellest part of it was the fact that the boys had gone a three-way split on a deal they were going to take with them. And when they got up there they were going to go out looking for magic mushies. Vlad's brother had given them directions to a little place past Mullumbimby where he said there was a carpet of mushrooms in the early morning.

"I promise. No smoking. No nothing. So why can't I go?" he'd yelled when Vlad and Thommo had gone. "Look, it was only one little joint. It's not like it was real drugs or anything. Why can't you be reasonable? I'm old enough to look after myself now."

No, his father and mother said. And so he had arrived at Mt Kuring-gai.

He was a storm cloud, thundering and dark: all he wanted was to be out of the place. Eileen had offered a cool drink just after he'd been dropped off by his father, four days before Christmas.

"Don't give me nothing," he had told her, "I don't want to be here, I don't want anything from anyone." Then he'd stormed up to the station to catch a train to the city and then out to Bondi. He wanted to get as far away as he could from the two old people he'd been dumped with. They were so boring. His grandfather spent nearly the whole day in the garden. How could anyone find enough to occupy himself for a whole day in a garden?

He sat too long on the beach, so his skin burned. In the senselessness of his rage he hadn't taken a hat, so his face and nose suffered particularly. But with nowhere else to go, he had to return to Mt Kuring-gai eventually. He didn't get back until nearly midnight, on the last train. He went straight to his room and banged the door after him. His grandparents, whose own bedtime had long since passed, got out of their bed where they weren't sleeping, and relievedly locked up.

Alex was tapped awake the next morning at six. His grandfather was at the bedroom door: "Come up the back with me."

Alex was wearing only short pyjama pants: "What do you mean?' he asked, "I haven't woken up yet."

"Put on some clothes and come up the back," Neil insisted.

"I want to go back to bed."

"No. You're coming with me." Alex didn't argue again with the craggy old man in the doorway. He pulled on jeans and a T-shirt.

They went up to the greenhouse. The rich smells of germination enveloped them as Neil slid the door open and they entered the little glass shed.

"You're a rude young bugger, aren't you," Neil said. He turned to a seeding tray he'd left the day before, emptying out some remnants of its last load, and beginning to fill it again with some potting mix he trowelled from a plastic bag.

"I didn't ask to come here." Alex had his arms folded across his chest. The smell and the heat were making him feel slightly nauseous.

"Yes, we've got that message loud and clear. You finished your HSC and wanted to go off with your mates to Byron Bay and prove you could act like an adult. So you think your behaviour yesterday was adult?"

"I don't know. I don't care."

"Eileen was very, very upset. She was worried you wouldn't come back. She thought you must be angry with her, given the history we've had with your father. You can't run out like that, Alex. You must let us know what you're doing. Can you pass me those secateurs?"

"I'm old enough to look after myself." He wished he had something else to say. It sounded repetitious, even to him. But he passed the secateurs.

"I don't doubt that. Do you think you could put some of these seeds in this tray? It'll help me a lot. We don't want to tell you what to do, you can be sure of that. If you want to go to the beach, that's fine. We just want to know where you are. A matter of courtesy."

"Yeah, well it wasn't me who lost my cool. Dad can be a real arsehole. It's not my fault he turned into an alkie. I mean, he was the one who had to go and have the treatment. All I did was get caught with a joint. And I didn't cause the fights he and Mum had. It was better when he did drink. How deep should I bury them in the dirt? This much? I ought to be able to look after myself. I feel like a little kid, everybody looking out for me. He's so goody two shoes now. He and Mum are so lovey dovey all the time since he's had counselling and they've finished their trial separation. I was really looking forward to Byron Bay. Not Mt Kuring-gai. Things here aren't exactly exciting for, you know, a young person, though you probably know that. Now do I splash some water over?"

"Just drip a fine mist. You'll wash them out if you tip too much water over them. Sorry we can't offer more excitement. Consider our point of view, though. We weren't expecting a guest for Christmas. Not that we mind having you at all. Eileen is over the moon. I think the last time your father let any of the kids stay up here was when your mother was in the hospital having you, and Kieran came out for a week. Eileen loved that. And he loved being here too, doing what you're doing. Though you're a lot better than a five year old was." The old man paused before he asked: "Heard from him at all lately?"

"No. He's just disappeared. We don't even talk about him at home any more. What are these going to grow into?"

"Columbines, those ones. Know them?"

"No."

"They're called granny bonnets sometimes. Pretty little things. I wonder what Kieran's doing for Christmas?"

"Dunno. But he'll probably send me a present. He's sent me one every birthday and Christmas since he went. Only me. No-one else." Alex felt he could tell Neil this. "He sent me Nikes last Christmas. Nothing yet though. He's always been early before. But don't tell Mum and Dad he's been doing that. They think the presents are from weird relatives Kieran invents. Well, he doesn't really invent them. They're people we don't see often. Like you. He put your name on one of them. Mum was going to ring you, but I told her I already had. Sorry. But he's a bit late this year. It could be because the post office is holding the mail."

"Maybe he's had a problem this year. He mightn't have had a chance to get you anything."

"Yeah. Or maybe he's got no money. I've been wondering how he paid for things. The Nikes he sent me last year would have cost $180."

"Well, sounds like you owe him a present."

"I dunno. Why should I owe him anything? You don't know what he did when he left. It was really gross."

"So he was rude too, was he? It must run in the family. Your father's never told us the details. But that helps me make my point. Do you reckon you can pay us the courtesy of telling us where you're going? It's Eileen who worries. It made her spend the whole day cooking you dinner, because she thinks it's her fault you took off like that."

"She didn't do anything. I just wanted to get some space. I'll tell her I'm sorry this morning."

"She'd appreciate that. Can you pass that packet of lime over?"

"What time do you have breakfast around here? I'm starving."

"It was a very nice dinner we had last night. Pity you missed it."

Alex took himself off to the beach that day too, but Neil and Eileen knew where he was going then. He took his hat, plenty of sunscreen, and didn't stay very long. There was a flower seller at the station on the way back, so he brought Eileen a bunch of flowers. She bustled to find a vase for them, to add to the many arrangements in the house from her own garden. He wondered whether he should have bought chocolates. He had planned to go to the beach the next day too. Even the hour and a half travelling there and back was worth it for the cool water and the waves. And, even by himself, perhaps more because of that, he enjoyed the view of the north end of the beach from behind his Ray-Bans. The topless girls turning like barbecued chooks in one of the takeaways on Campbell Parade, but a much more mouth watering sight. But his grandfather asked him over a roast chicken dinner whether he would help with the finishing of some toys for the Community Centre Christmas tree, and Alex surprised himself by saying yes.

Breasts. Tanned breasts. The breasts of Alyson Ford had not seen as much sun. Her skin was paler, that easy burning freckly type. And very different when touched to what he expected. His experience of breasts was that they were hard, like his own muscle, or like the bodies of boys at football. But his experience was limited to breasts in brassieres, bound and fixed behind tube tops or tight dresses, and furtive hands moving over them when kissing at parties. He had had one seriously passionate evening with Shradtha when her parents had gone to see a touring Indian singer. The two of them were supposed to be studying mathematics and modern history, but biology took over. He'd felt under the straps of her bra, and she'd moved her fingers over his underpants. They'd even tongue-kissed, but that was just when her parents were pulling into the driveway.

Maybe he should, after all, ease the pressure in his pyjama pants.

There is a tap on the bedroom door: "Alex, are you awake yet?" His grandfather wants company with his early morning cuppa.

Eileen doesn't get up until 7.30, when it is the routine for Neil to let the old dog Hugo stumble his way out from the kitchen up to their bedroom. Eileen would be brought to consciousness with a faceful of hairy halitosis. The dog has lost the strength to jump right up on the bed, as it had done since it was a pup, and now can stretch only as far as Eileen's face asleep upon her handmade lace pillow. She seems to enjoy this horror of awakenings, always making affectionate noises towards the arthritic spaniel. He is sixteen years old. Almost as old as Alex is, for God's sake. But going blind, and a menace at meal times when he lies under the table and farts.

Alex and Neil have fallen into this pattern in the few weeks Alex has been staying at Mt Kuring-gai. It is a quiet and meditative beginning to the day. It creates an order and pattern, an ordinary foundation upon which chaotic events can then unfold almost as if they were everyday occurrences. He has come to welcome the quiet companionship he and Neil share in the quiet morning. He answers his grandfather with sufficient noise for the old man's deafening ears to hear, and pushes himself out of bed. His erection is already subsiding. He puts on a dressing gown nevertheless.

Neil has gone back to the kitchen. Alex hurries through the house, past the half open door of the room where Eileen sleeps, to meet him. When he opens the kitchen door, Hugo shuffles to his feet to make a half-hearted attempt to come and sniff good morning. Alex reaches the straggly creature before his creaky old bones can lever him fully up. He scratches Hugo behind the ears and the dog flops back down into semi-slumber. Hugo sleeps most of these days.

Neil pours hot water into the teapot. He has put out two mugs, one of which is quickly in Alex's hands. The cup and gesture, the silence, is the same as that afternoon at Alyson's. Alex sniffed at the tea. Neil's usual Bushells. Alyson had made Earl Grey. Alex liked that tea, the smoky aroma of which was another reminder of that Thursday of last week. But he sips Neil's less fragrant brew nevertheless.

They had both still been naked. She had told him, "Get dressed. You'll have to go now."

"Why?" he asked. "You're the one who dragged me here. What if I don't want to go?"

"I've got things to do now Alex. Don't act like a silly boy with me. Just do what you're told, o.k.? Enjoy it and dream about it until something nicer comes along. But just remember, this was the way we mourned him."

Mourning. Even in the middle of her passion she was mourning. On top of him, groaning, grabbing at him, biting his nipples, she was mourning. Had he been mourning? She remained naked while he dressed. She sat on the sofa, sipping her tea and looking at a *House and Garden.* It hurt, the way she no longer cared about him after what they'd done. He had wanted her to find him attractive, to be close to him, to fall in love, like his brother had shown he had done in his notebook. Though in his writing there his brother had also revealed he had enjoyed sex without love, just for the pleasure of it, so maybe Alex could as well.

Alyson had a weatherboard house in Leichhardt. Her bedroom was up a flight of stairs, right under the roof. The air was thick and liquid, specks of dust floating on the layers of heat. When they had been up there they'd left the windows at each end open for the air to flow through while they'd stroked and been kind to each other on her brass bed. On the street, after she'd closed the door behind him without another kiss, he'd hitched his bag over a shoulder and begun the trudge to the bus stop on Marion Street. It was either a noise or a feeling that made him turn. He would never know exactly what. She was reaching out to close the window. She'd let her hair down so that the strands fell and curled under her bare breasts. The breasts themselves hung down, delicate and pear-like. So different to the flattened saucers he marvelled at when he was inside her, she lying on her back with her legs twisted behind his. He'd waved at her. He'd thought she was up there to wave goodbye to him. But she'd been too intent on closing the window to notice him.

"It's going to be a real hot one." Neil stares out past the verandah into the back yard, where a few birds are already pecking on the grass. "Got anything planned for the day?" he continues, still without looking at Alex.

"Nothing special. Do you need any help?"

"I'd welcome whatever you can offer."

"No probs. I wouldn't be able to borrow the car a bit later would I? Thought I better get some stuff for home. Milk and bread and things. Eileen suggested it."

"That's a good idea. The lawn'll need mowing too. Maybe I better come with you, just to see everything's the way your mother and father would expect it. Wouldn't want them to come back and blame us for anything would we? But you can drive. It'll be good to sit back and let someone else do it for me."

"You hate my driving. You're always petrified when I drive you."

"You're getting better. Slowly but surely. Your father, Robert, he damn near did me in once when I was teaching him to drive, you know. Accelerated going around a corner. I had to grab the wheel off him or we'd have gone right up a big gum tree."

"He hasn't improved."

"No. That's why he drives that Volvo," the old man laughs.

Alex eyes his grandfather through the steam of a raised tea mug. He smiles at the weak joke. And smiles at his grandfather, the gruff, taciturn gardener. That was what Neil now was, but Alex could see also the young Flight-Sergeant in his baggy flying suit calmly flying a stricken Lancaster back to base. In the few weeks he'd spent with Neil, Alex has come to know the man in all his manifestations, though most of these he hides so that he appears simply as a gardener. Even now, the profile of Neil's face in the sharp semi-light of morning, is closed, the ridges of his brows shadowy. The skin of his face and arms is tanned by the sun he spends large parts of the day in. Dark spots on his forehead are signs of the damage the sun has done. His hands are big, both of them now cradling his tea mug. He has rough, hard-worked fingers, dried scaly from too much handling of phosphate and lime. There are a number of nails turned brown from dried blood underneath where a hammer or other tool has once bruised.

"He loves his Volvos," Alex says quietly. "He could pick a worse car, I guess."

"No he couldn't," his grandfather answers, and they both chuckle. It is a long-running joke: everybody knows that the only people who drive Volvos can't. Alex continues to sip at his tea. The birds are well awake now, their songs clear and vibrant even inside the kitchen. Long, drawled croaks, sharp caws, bell-like cascades, with the drone of cicadas, the familiar overture to a Sydney summer day.

Alex would have liked to tell Neil he was going to Alyson Ford's place. To work up a sweat in her bed. Lick down between her legs, taste again the salty, moist flesh of her lower lips. Spread them with his tongue.

Better than ice-cream, down there. Caviar, oysters and roe. The salt and sweaty taste of the folds of her body. And with a face as juiced as after eating a mango. Lick the hair away from her vulva; go face first like a bee into her orchid.

"Got a lot of cymbidiums I want to split up and repot before it gets too hot. I can take some down to Turramurra as a present for your mother. She likes them." Neil begins to stand up. His back hurts him now, but he can still put in a day's work that leaves Alex exhausted. He has a belly on him, but overall he is more solid than fat. For a man of seventy, he is in pretty good shape. Past that rough surface, Alex knows there is a man whom he would not be ashamed to be. His grandfather, he knows now, is a man who is not frightened of being afraid, and a man who does not need to speak of his faith because his faith has become unshakeable and unbreakable. And he is a man who has seen Hell, and knows it is possible to return from it. Alex knows because Alex and Neil have been to Hell together. For Alex, the journey has been just a few days. But for Neil, the journey has taken a lifetime.

Some long days have passed, Alex thinks as he enjoys the refill of tea Neil had poured him without even asking. When Alex's mother and father had driven him up here just three weeks before, he had not expected to be still hanging around. He had had plans to take off. He was going to hitch up to Byron. There was no way he was going to suffer a summer repenting one little joint he hadn't even smoked. Now, he reflected, here he was, and enjoying himself.

Less than a month ago, he had been expecting a horror like Brewarrina. There, his grandmother, his mother's mother, had had him and, at first, Kieran for several summers.

The first time, when Alex was twelve, it had been an experience in independence. A place where he and his brother had finally established a rapport. The chance to develop a united front for mutual survival. Their grandmother loved her grandsons, but herself had borne only daughters. And, after that, the boys' elder sisters had stayed with her. The girls had been so good. They helped with the cooking. They always washed up. They made their own beds. They went to church with her. But boys were a foreign thing to her. Being foreign meant having to accept her ways completely, because only her ways were the right ways. Anything foreign was wrong. And dirty. And in need of constant correction. Which made the boys want to spend as much time as they could away from her. Both Alex and Kieran had had the foresight to take their bicycles. From morning until as late in the evening as the light would let them they rode far into the spaces where their grandmother had not walked and left traces of her female smells.

After one especially sharp morning when Nanna had sat Alex down and fiercely brushed his hair flat with some hair tonic she'd unearthed from somewhere, and then threatened to do the same with Kieran, the brothers rode away into the sparse landscape, flushed with their indignity.

"She wouldn't do it to Lisa," Alex had finally said.

"Yes, she would. But Lisa would let her. And she'd say 'thank you Nanna'."

"Why does she pick on us?"

"Why do any of them?" Kieran began to relate a story from when he was seven. Alex had been still too small to be let loose with his brother and sisters. Tracey and Lisa had been wrestling with Kieran. It was Lisa, four years older and with the weight of age, who had pinned Kieran down and proceeded to spit in his face. First in his eyes, then on his mouth, then all over until she'd run out of saliva and let him up to run off and wash his face.

"That's yuck. Why did she do that?"

"Because I was a boy."

"Well, you could get her back now. You're bigger'n her. You could spit on her."

"Yeah, yeah. That'd go down real well. Anyway, it doesn't matter. That happened when we were kids. I've got over it. I reckon Lisa would die if I told that story in front of her friends."

"You could do that. They're all stuck-up snobs."

"I just might, someday. It'll keep. But, Jeez, I wish I could get out of this place. This town is so dead."

Kieran was deeply resentful of Brewarrina. Alex remembers that. Kieran was seventeen then too. But their grandmother particularly doted on him, her first grandson. She had nagged at her daughter to have Kieran sent up to her for two weeks after Christmas every year for years. And her daughter had obliged. Kieran had been to Brewarrina with Lisa once, and with Tracey a couple of times. Then for three years on his own, before Alex was considered old enough to go as well.

"Nanna is the big problem. How can I get this gunk out of my hair. Californian Poppy. Yech!"

"Alex, you are my salvation. When I've been here before, I've had Nanna and Lisa or Tracey trying that out on me. Nanna has even tried to make me wear a tie."

"A tie? Out here? What for?"

"She'll start on you, so be prepared. Gentlemen wear ties and collars. 'Scruff' wear singlets and T-shirts. Can I have the water bottle, please?"

In the flat landscape, the years between them filtered away. Alex started throwing rocks at birds. After a surreptitious check of the horizon, Kieran joined his younger brother. When he finally hit a crow, which cawed alarmingly and staggered slightly before regaining its dignity, he called an end to the game and suggested they ride on further.

"How have you coped with Nanna all these years?" Alex asked as they slowly pedalled nowhere. "She's so strict."

"You just have to agree with her," Kieran answered as they rested in some rare shade. "She'll do anything for you if you're polite and accept what she has to say. It's not too much to ask is it? She thinks she's passing on wisdom or something. I dunno. I just say 'Yes, Grandma' and leave it at that. But don't let her find a spoof stain on your sheet."

"What?" Alex still remembered the surprise he had felt when Kieran suddenly started talking about sex. He had been uncomfortable at first. He had secrets he hadn't shared with anyone.

"Don't wank on her sheets! The year before last, I was dragged down to the laundry and had to scrub with bleach and soap to get a stain off a sheet. I can't even remember doing it. I think it must have been a wet dream. I was sleeping out on the verandah, under the mozzie screens. It was nice and cool out there. I'd decided I wasn't going to wear pyjamas any more. That must have been how it happened. Course I'd been damn careful to wank in the bathroom or dunny or somewhere outside where I could wash it away. She really lay down the law on that one. 'Spilling seed' she called it. I was amazed she even knew what it was."

"But isn't it going to cause some damage if you let all the white stuff come out like that?" Alex had asked.

Kieran raised his eyebrows: "You think wanking is going to hurt you?"

"I don't know. I'm asking."

"You've played with your stiff, though."

"Yeah, yeah. Lot's of times. But not to, you know."

"Not to shoot."

"Yeah."

"Have you got hair yet?"

"Not much. Maybe I should have more. It's funny. It's tough stuff down there."

Kieran laughed: "Yeah. Like wire. Real bad when it gets stuck between your teeth."

"What?" Alex didn't understand what Kieran meant then, but it had been something he remembered later.

"Never mind. Just a joke. Here." Kieran suddenly undid his shorts and dropped them. His thick footballer's thighs were tanned brown, but he was white from below his belly button to the tops of his thighs. He was wearing red bikini briefs which were smaller than the white strip where the sun had not touched. He flipped the top of the briefs down to show his pubic hair. "This is what mine looks like. Yours is probably pretty much the same. It is with most guys I know." He pulled his pants back up again.

"Yeah, mine is pretty much like that. Just not as much."

"Well, have you ever come at all."

"I reckon I've had wet dreams. Like I've wet myself. It woke me up. I was scared. I didn't know how I could tell Mum. But it was only a little bit. In the morning it had dried and my pyjamas were stuck to my skin. Then I thought something must have broken, because I had all this dried stuff on my stomach. I didn't know what to do then."

"Bet you kept going and checking it every hour to make sure it hadn't fallen off, or done something else funny."

"Yeah, I did."

"Me too, when it first happened. Then I realised it was perfectly normal. And I could make it happen when I wanted to. So I started wanking till I came."

"And nothing's happened?"

"Look. No hair on my palms. And I'm not mad either. Not so's you'd notice anyway."

"I notice all right."

"Hey. Show some respect. I'm bigger that you after all."

"Yeah. You are. How come I'm so scrawny? Were you like this when you were my age?"

"I was always big. The tallest in the class. Which isn't always good, you know. So don't let being smaller than me get you down, kid. Things change really quickly. You mightn't think so now, but you'll think differently when you're my age."

"But what did you think when you were my age? I'm going to be a puny, weak wuz. You could never have thought that."

"But, Alex, you've got to work at things. I've had to do a lot of running to keep fit."

"That's great for you. You've always been good at sport. I try to play cricket and rugby, but you can see the guys looking at me knowing they could have someone better on their team. I can't catch for peanuts. I'm a poof when it comes to catching."

Kieran was silent for a moment: "All I can say is practice makes perfect. You practise the catching, you'll get better at it. Of course I like playing. I like sport. I like keeping fit. Not everyone wants to play sport. That's okay. It doesn't matter so long as you're happy with what you're doing. There's no point in being miserable in life. There's nothing wrong with your body. It's yours. That's the most important thing. Mine is mine, and I like it. But if you had it, I don't think you'd be happy."

"Huh?"

"Everybody's normal, Alex. It's just that everybody's different as well. What would be the fun if we were all the same as each other?"

The brothers sat silently in the shade for some moments. Then Alex found the time was right to ask his brother for some advice: "How do you wank?"

"Me? Personally? Or is that a more general question?"

"You. When I tried it, I use my hand — like this." Alex clenched his fist, and demonstrated his stroke. "Is that how you do it?"

"Mostly, yeah. Sometimes I use spit, or soap, or some oil. Or rub. I guess it's whatever makes you feel good. You going to become a mad wanker now?"

"No. I just wondered how you did it. It's something you find out by yourself, isn't it. It's not something you get a lesson in." Kieran had found that very funny, though he didn't say why. But from then on, Alex had been able to talk to Kieran about things. Things which, when he had tried to talk about them with his father, had brought forward the response: "What do you want to know that for?" The closeness they'd established dissipated once they arrived back in Sydney. Kieran was immediately back in the company of his friends, and Alex had his own crowd. Yet, back at school, little differences were noticeable. Kieran didn't take Alex to his first day at High School, and he hardly ever acknowledged him if he saw him in the playground. The Seniors had their own area, anyway. But one day, about two weeks into first term, Alex found himself being pushed around by two Year 9 boys as he was walking his bike out of the gate.

"Give us a dollar," one of them said, "or we'll bash you."

"Fuck off," Alex said.

He was punched in the back, hard.

"Give us a dollar."

"No!"

Alex tried to push his bike past the two, but they grabbed it and held him still: "Now you're gunner get it," the other one said.

"No, he's not," Kieran said. He had walked up behind the bullies and they turned to find his school captain's badge smiling at them. "You two better fuck off now. I suggest you quit this racket. But if you keep it up, just make sure you leave my brother right out of it. O.K.?"

The bullies nodded and scurried off.

"You're alright, aren't you mate?" Kieran continued to Alex. "Just get on your bike and ride straight home. I reckon they're too chicken to try anything else, but you never know." Kieran was right. There was no further trouble. And for the one year they were at school together Alex was comforted that Kieran was watching out for him.

But then Kieran was gone. Not only from school, but from home as well. A person, a topic, to be discussed no longer. And, if she couldn't have Kieran, Nanna wanted Alex up with her. At thirteen, Brewarrina had just been bearable. Grandma, all good intentions, was a little too curious about her now vanished favourite grandson. Alex just repeated the lie his mother had given him; Kieran had chosen to go overseas before he started university.

At thirteen it seemed to Alex Nanna went to bed too early, though in reality no earlier than a year before. She kept wondering to him all the time why Kieran hadn't sent her as much as a postcard. She even rang their mother to check Kieran was safe. The daughter had used the cordless phone well, wandering around the empty house in Sydney while she continued to flow the stream of white lies to her mother in Brewarrina. On this occasion, the daughter could not find the words to tell her mother the truth. But it was Alex who had had to be face to face with the disappointed old woman.

When he was fifteen, he had begged his parents not to send him away to her. He would die there, he said. Grandma insisted he be in bed by 8.30. She cooked lamb chops and vegies six nights a week and had fish fingers — fish fingers! — on Fridays. She wouldn't let him drink coffee, not even Nescafe, which she didn't have anyway. She only had Bushells tea. She made it so strong you could hardly drink it. Dipped her Arnott's Morning Tea biscuits in it. For too long. When he helped her wash up, the sodden crumbs in the bottom of the cup would mingle with the coagulated lamb fat in the aluminium strainer she placed under the sink-plug. The water would be blocked. Then he had to pull the mess out with his fingers. She made him wash. She insisted on drying because she knew where to put things away, and it was good training for him, anyway, for when he was married.

That was the year something had happened to him there that he still dreamed about. He'd wake in the middle of the night, those events still so clear in his mind, and his mind so unclear about why the dream was so strong.

He had gone off wandering, to get away from Grandma. Like Kieran before him, he'd found the best thing to do was simply to disappear. She'd rouse when he got back, but not for long. He had his bike with him again, and he'd ridden down a rough, dirt track, his

Walkman attached to his belt with the speaker leads twining up his chest to his ears. He'd found a sandy bend in the river where he'd sat down and started to draw things in the sand. Doodles. Nothing more than lines. Maybe he was thinking about breasts and vaginas, maybe about his own body, maybe he wasn't thinking about anything at all. Just scratching shapes in the sand while Nirvana poured into his ears.

A shadow fell across his stick scrawling in the sand. A quick, startled look showed him he was surrounded by a group of Aboriginal boys. They'd come up on him easily, with his eyes intent on his sand drawing and his ears full of guitars and drums. Immediately, he was scared. His grandmother, all her life in Brewarrina, had no nice words for the indigenous people. And he'd never been this close to so many of them, so close to them and so far from anyone who could help him.

"Whatcha drawing?' one of them asked.

"Nothing." He started to kick away his scribblings, embarrassed that these boys might be able to read more into them than had ever been meant.

""Hey, you been thinking about rooting, eh." The biggest of them was examining the drawings closely. "Look at this. He's got this woman here already, and this big dick about to fuck her." The boy was laughing as he told the story in the sand to the others, who enjoyed his interpretation.

"What's ya name?" he asked Alex. "Can I ride ya bike?" another asked. "What's the music you're listening to?" A younger boy had come up close to Alex and was trying to hear the sound coming out of the earphones, now hanging round his neck. Alex detached the Walkman and let the kid listen to it. By then they were a group, and he was part of them, ambling by the river. There were fish traps close by. Stone dams that the boys told Alex their forefathers had built way back, in the Dreaming when the world was being made. They moved along the traps, knee-deep in water, hands searching for fish. Nobody caught any, nobody trying too hard.

They'd taken a detour over a headland where Kevin, the oldest, had followed the tracks of a kangaroo. There were too many of them, too noisy, and without weapons, to be effective hunters. But the amiable jaunt brought them back to a deep pool in the river.

Alex was disconcerted by the freedom with which the group flung away their clothes and threw themselves into the Barwon. He had skinny-dipped before, but that had been furtively at night, a quick dip in a friend's pool after the two of them had drunk an illicit six-pack of beer. He was slow to remove his clothes, but quick to enter the water, where his new friends surrounded him, ducked him, splashed him, wound him into a strange game of diving for a white rock. He soon forgot he was naked.

They group had made its decision to leave the water and dry in the sun after a hectic forty minutes or so. They'd sat in a row on the sand, each one seeming to have his place, even Alex, fitted in between Kevin and a darker, quieter boy they called Maggot. Kevin had a cigarette he lit and passed down the line. Alex took a small puff — he knew his grandmother would smell smoke on him — and passed it to Maggot. Their arms brushed together.

"You're white all right," Maggot noted in his deep mumble. Maggot's skin was very brown, almost black, smooth, with a blue sheen to it as the water steamed off.

Alex's own skin was pale, and already pink from exposure to too much sun, blond down on his arms: "I wish I had skin like yours," he told Maggot.

"No, you don't," Maggot breathed a stream of tobacco smoke into Alex's face. "No whitey would wish for skin like mine." His voice was so soft, no-one else seemed to hear him. But his eyes had locked with Alex's as he had spoken, sad eyes. These Alex would dream about.

And about the young boy, Robbie, who had put back on the Walkman and moved in front of the row of boys. He was staring closely at Alex's cock: "Are you cut mate?"

"Yeah." Alex's throat was dry, the smoking only part of the cause.

"I'm not," Robbie said, which was obvious as he picked up his own cock between finger and thumb and examined it. He pulled the skin back to show his pink knob. "See?"

"In the old days," said Kevin, "they used to cut and do things to the boys when we got old enough. A sharp bit of rock to slice the skin off, maybe a few slits they might fill up with clay or something like that to make big scars. There's some old men I seen got those things on them. Looks bloody ugly, eh. And musta hurt like nothing else."

"Did it hurt you?" Robbie asked Alex.

"I dunno. I was anaesthetised. There was something wrong with me when I was three. Apparently I couldn't roll the skin back, so I had to go and get it cut off."

"When you were three. Were you awake?"

"I'm not sure. I don't remember much. I think I was. I dream I was."

"Yeah?" Kevin said. "Course, the old fellas, they say it hurt a whole lot, but when it came to lovemaking, not only did it feel real good for them, but those scars and bumps drove the women wild so they'd want it all night. Maybe those old fellas knew something after all, eh." The sympathy pains Alex was feeling in his groin for that long ago event eased somewhat in the following laughter, then were totally relieved by the group's decision to break up and head for home. Robbie returned Alex's Walkman with a request that he be able to borrow it again next time they met.

They never did meet again.

His grandmother had smelt the smoke. She had been prepared to be indulgent about the young and their vices until he had mentioned that he'd spent some time with the boys. She'd become very angry, and made him have a bath. He'd had to soap himself thoroughly then submit to her pouring disinfectant in the water.

"All sorts of diseases in that community," she told him. "You'd better wash your hair, too. I'll get some lotion for lice. What would your mother say if I sent you home with nits and the rest of it. Don't you go near any of those people ever again. You hear me?"

Nanna and disinfectant. She would clean the world of all the badness she perceived in it, if she could. What would she have done to Kieran, Alex thought. What would she have done if her daughter had not lied about Kieran's disappearance? If Alex had been sent to Brewarrina instead of Mt Kuring-gai, the world would not be what it was now. He would not have had his afternoon in Leichhardt. He would not be sipping tea at six in the morning and enjoying it. He would not be peacefully at ease in his grandfather's company. He would not have buried his brother. All for a joint he had left in his pocket. And it wasn't even good stuff.

Tomorrow, he thinks, I could meet a girl who'd do what Bronwyn did. Or I could be smashed to pieces on the freeway.

"Alex?" Neil asks. "Did you hear me? Do you think it'd be a good idea for me to prepare some cymbidiums for your mother."

"Great. I like the flowers on those. There's something very sensual about them. They're like the lips of a vagina."

Neil stares at his grandson in surprise: "I hadn't thought that myself, but you're right. You've got a bit of the poet in you Alex. Funny thing is orchids are named orchids because the bulbs are supposed to look like testicles."

"Then they are very sexy plants, aren't they?" Alex finishes the last of his tea.

"I reckon you could say that." His grandfather stretches to his full height: "This time tomorrow, we'll be half way to Kingsford-Smith. You ready for that?" Ready? Ready to meet his parents on their return from Bali? Ready to tell his mother and father what had happened?

It was only one week since Alex had been with Alyson Ford. Only eight days since the funeral. He didn't know what he was ready for.

"I have absolutely no idea, Neil. What about you?"

"We'll see what the day brings won't we. Come on, let's get to work."

Thursday, December 24, 1992
Mt Kuring-gai, Australia
10.34 a.m.

Neil and Alex had spent much of the bright blue morning up in the greenhouse, bathed in the rich, fecund scent of moist earth which was germinating the myriad seeds Neil had set into his seeding boxes. They had been working mostly without speaking. The tasks had become routine in little more than an hour. Neil would occasionally cast an eye over Alex's work and suggest a minor change. But their work had a rhythm to it even in their silence.

Alex was flecked with burnt skin peeling from his face, arms and legs. From time to time, the itchiness was too much to bear, and he scratched. Clawed streaks of dirt showed. He started to scratch again. His neck was particularly sensitive.

"Leave it, Alex," Neil said. "You'd be better to put some cream on. And you should have taken sunscreen with you when you took off."

"Yeah. And I should have worn a hat."

"You should have. Very poor planning. Live and learn eh. Are you going to go off to the beach today? If you do, you make sure you put on lots of sunscreen. Lots of it. I don't want to explain to your mother and father why I let you burn yourself to a crisp."

"It was my fault. I take all the responsibility. I was stupid. I shouldn't have done it. I'm a silly, immature seventeen year old. We do these stupid things. Didn't you ever do anything like that?"

"We all do stupid things. At your age, I was trying to get myself killed, and I thought I was doing it for honour and glory."

"What do you mean?"

"The war was beginning when I was seventeen. The biggest thing that had ever happened in my life. I wanted to play my part. I did everything I could to get into the Empire Air Training Scheme. That had been set up to make sure enough pilots were being trained for the air force. We worked really closely with the Brits then. They thought they had a bloody empire, but the only notice they ever took of us was when they were in trouble. So the Canadians and the New Zealanders and us were all part of this scheme to provide Mother England with enough pilots to replace all the ones who were getting killed. The Germans had better planes then, you see. Better planes and better pilots. Of course, I didn't know any of that then. And it wasn't something the recruiters were going to let on. 'You'll see the world' they said. 'A six-month trip, twelve at the most, all paid for. You'll go to places you've only dreamed about.

Meet scores of girls. And you'll fly!' It was a good yarn and I fell for it. And I did want to see the world. The war meant travel, exotic places, girls and everything that was different and better than life on a dairy farm. The funny thing was working on a dairy farm meant I could have stayed safely at home. But I couldn't bear being a farm boy any longer"

"Weren't you at all afraid of being killed?"

"Were you afraid of getting sunburnt?"

"I didn't think about it."

"And I didn't think about getting killed."

"But the danger was obvious."

"No it wasn't. We were going to fight for right. For freedom. Those low-down Nazis hadn't played cricket and now it was time to tell them that Britannia really ruled the waves. That's how it was put to us. And then there were the uniforms which started the girls taking notice of us. Besides, they said, by the time we finished our training and got over there, it'd all be over. We could drink French wine, flirt with the mademoiselles, eat Belgian chocolate, smoke lots of Capstans and prepare to head home as heroes. Of course it wasn't like that and I was stupid to think there was any truth in the propaganda they put out. It was all lies. All lies told to get us to go and fight. Like in any war. The poor dumb soldiers are supposed to be content to line up for the slaughtering. To do the bidding of the fat cats who run the world. I should have known. But I was young and stupid, ready to believe their lies. And it was also what I was expected to do. A lot of pressure was put on us young blokes to sign up. The ones who wear the suits were telling us it was the right thing to do. No-one questions them. They've got to be right, don't they, because they run the country. Like a fool, I believed them. I signed up to do their dirty work. My father didn't agree, though."

"But the Nazis and the Japanese were trying to destroy Australia. The Nazis were killing Jews and invading France and stuff."

"Yes they were. The Nazis were pretty sick people all right, but who had encouraged them to think they could rule Europe? The English had. The English King, whatsisname, the one who married the divorced American, he even met with the Nazis. And, sure, they were bad, but wasn't segregation in America as bad? The Americans even had separate black and white fighting units. And in Chicago and places like that the corruption in the cities was as bad, maybe is still as bad, as the distorted way the Nazis looked at the world. As for the Japanese, they had been carving out their little co-prosperity sphere in East Asia. The history books all tell you they were brutal imperialists, but don't forget what France was doing in Indochina, Belgium and England were doing in Africa, and America was doing in the Philippines. The Japanese were no worse than any of the white powers. Their only problem was they weren't white. They wanted an empire to give them markets and raw materials just like the English had. But the Americans hemmed them in. Denied them oil. So they had little choice other than to attack Pearl Harbour. Don't get me wrong. I'm not excusing the Nazis or the Japanese. I'm just saying no-one was necessarily so good they could call themselves better. Here, we locked up Jewish refugees because we were frightened of their difference. As for that Churchill man, he was prepared to have our troops fight in some tactical campaign in Africa while the Japanese invaded us. And the Americans, they were everywhere with their money and machinery. They took over the whole war and then took over the whole world. And look what happened! The Japanese are finally in Australia. They didn't have to come with armies and guns. They only had to come with pocketsful of yen, and we rushed to sell the country to them. Are they any different now to then, do you reckon?"

"They had the atom bomb dropped on them."

"Yes, the Americans did that. A horrible weapon. But I don't think the Japanese have really changed. It's how we see them that has changed. In the war we portrayed them as little yellow devils, with glasses and sharp teeth. They had one aim in mind, and that was to rape our women. Now, they seem like reasonable blokes, and we let them rape our country. Let them cut down all our forests so some slimy suit can put more money in his bank account. All for the short term. We're so stupid, Alex. We just don't understand our country. We let short-sighted, greedy developers and entrepreneurs kid us that they're doing good for the country when we know they're really destroying it. We let them walk through the holes in the law to turn this fragile land into a dustbowl. And the really sad thing is we know we're doing it and we don't stop it. We even vote these creeps into Parliament. We give them the responsibility to devastate our forests, mine our beaches and to send young men off to war. They had no compunction in sending some of our sailors over to the Persian Gulf when that little debacle was going on last year. And they would have sent more if things had gone differently. Those people in government, they talk only to business. It's all economics. All money. They simply don't see the people."

"Gee, Neil, I didn't realise you were so radical. You talk like a revolutionary or something. You get more worked up than dad when he's giving one of his 'how great Gough Whitlam was' speeches."

"I'm not a revolutionary. I'm just a simple ordinary bloke. I went off to a stupid war and saw I was just a pawn in a game played by those with the money, the ones who really run this world. All I wanted to do when I got back from the war was live a simple life. Keep out of the way of the big boys. Plants like these ones here don't know how to be greedy, or how to rip off other living things. Little children don't know that either. That's why I like making toys for them, and being Santa."

"But children can be mean and horrible. Trust me. I've not long finished being one."

"Yes, we teach them that because that's what they see everyday. On television they see that greed pays."

"I don't know. I've watched a lot of television. But I don't think I'm too greedy."

"No, Alex, you're not too bad. A little silly, maybe. Getting sunburned like that. But you've done o.k. over the past couple of days. I know it can't be easy to be dumped here with us. But we are enjoying you being here."

"It's a lot better than I thought. I have to apologise to you, too, for being so rude when I arrived. I was so angry with Mum and Dad. I like being here, but I still don't see why I couldn't have gone to Byron. I wouldn't have done anything that wasn't being done by everybody else up there."

"That's a convoluted way of saying you'd have got into all the mischief you and your mates could think of."

"Yeah. But you would've, too, when you were our age, wouldn't you."

"I think so. And never mind the consequences."

"Well, I reckon you have to suffer for your fun a little. Like a hangover or something."

"Maybe. Could be worse. You could hurt yourself. More than getting sunburned. You could damage your mind with drugs."

"Come on, Neil. I had a little joint in my pocket. Marijuana doesn't hurt you."

"You know for sure?"

"Don't do this to me. I don't want a big lecture about drugs. I know all the dangers. I don't want to touch anything I have to inject, or anything like that. That sort of stuff scares me. But I'm really like you. I'm really just ordinary. Normal."

"You seem like that, Alex. And you've been doing a good job here. And I reckon those toys we took down to the Community Centre yesterday were pretty good. You did a very nice paint job on them. They were a bit younger looking than if I'd done them. I'm not really into the abstract stuff."

"I could tell. You didn't say anything when you saw my train engine, but the way you looked at it, I could tell."

"The kids liked it though. That's what's important."

"Yeah."

Alex finished his work on a tray of seeds. He stepped out of the shed into the back garden. It was a another perfect summer day. The beach would be packed. Give it a few days and he'd be back. Now, the cloudless sky stretched empty above the suburban silence. Then crows cawing; in Mt Kuring-gai, they still did, not like in other crowded parts of the city. Braaaak. Braaaak. Braaaak. The heat restricted movement. The humidity, too. It was like walking through water; slow, effortful moving. Eileen came out of the house carrying a tray of biscuits and tea to the shaded table under the banksia rose. Snuffling Hugo at her heels, too scared to lose her rapidly fading scent in case that was the end of him, as well. Alex started brushing the potting mix from flowered cyclamens, preparing new and bigger pots for them to lie fallow in. Neil was breaking open the dead blossoms of gerberas and tweaking out the fluffy seeds.

"Tea or cordial, Alex?" Eileen called.

"Tea," he replied. Immediately. Without even thinking about it. He smiled. He was fitting in here. He'd better get down to the chemist this afternoon and get some sunscreen and some cream for his burnt skin. Otherwise he'd end up here everyday. A few days was alright, but there was no way he was going to waste all summer hanging around with his grandparents, nice as they were.

"Tea's up," Eileen announced. Alex and Neil put down their tools and joined her at the little table. Hugo burbled out a long stream of smelly wind. "Oh dear," said Eileen, "Just as well we're outside."

Alex smiled again, and took a biscuit from the tray.

"More tea?" Eileen asked. "I won't ask if you want any more biscuits. You've eaten nearly the whole plate."

"I only got one," Neil said.

"*I* only got one. You had two and Alex had the rest. It's alright for him, though. He's still growing. You need to shrink."

"Hmmm," Neil said.

"Nice biscuits," Alex said.

"I made them especially for Christmas. We haven't told you what we have to do tomorrow, have we dear."

"I was waiting for the right moment," Neil said. "It hadn't come yet."

"It has now. Alex, you haven't heard from your brother Kieran for a while have you?"

"No. I was telling Neil. He remembers every birthday and Christmas, but I haven't heard anything this year."

"Eileen's starting to tell you something I should have told you the other day. We actually have something for you from Kieran. It's not really a present, though."

"Yes, it is," Eileen said. "A present from the heart."

"You've heard from Kieran?" Alex asked.

"Well, we've been hearing from him ever since, you know, the argument at home." Neil was embarrassed to continue.

"You know what happened?"

"Kieran came here that night," Neil continued a little more easily. "He didn't know where else to go. He was here for a few days before he found a place with some friends in the city."

"He told you what had happened between him and Dad?"

"Yes, he did. I have to say I'm surprised at your father. His own flesh and blood. Throwing him out like that."

"But Kieran said he was —" Alex looked across at Eileen, who nodded at him to continue, "a poof — a homosexual. Dad had no choice except to chuck him out."

Alex was uncomfortable defending his father. That had been the night of the big row. Alex had been sent to his room. In the morning Kieran had left, and no-one spoke any more about him.

"Why?' asked Eileen.

Alex remembered it all very clearly. That evening, a Saturday, had been planned as a family gathering for his mother's birthday. Both of his sisters had come early. Tracey was there with Boris, whom she lived with in a small flat near the university where they were both studying to be teachers. Lisa was with a dork named Phil. After Kieran, she dumped him.

There was a table of dips, chips, olives and pate set up in the family room. It was April so, while the light still remained, the balcony doors were open. Phil and Boris were out on the balcony having a beer and admiring the view over the bush. It had grown back with tenacious resourcefulness since the January bushfires the year before.

Alex was watching television, the volume turned down every time Tracey, Lisa or his mother yelled from the kitchen that it was too loud, and gently increased until they yelled again.

Then Kieran had came home.

"Is he alright?" Alex asked.

Neil and Eileen looked at each other. Neil said: "No, he's not."

After Kieran had gone everything had changed. First, his mother wouldn't let Alex go anywhere by himself. Then the arguments between Mum and Dad started. They were never directly over Kieran.

"We don't want Alex turning out like that," his father would say when his mother was making sure Alex wouldn't come home from football practice alone.

"A good role model would have helped," she'd answer, "one who wasn't always drunk." His father had always drunk, but after Kieran had gone he'd tuck into the sherry as soon as he came home, and finish with scotches in his study after dinner. He ran out of scotch one night and drove up to the pub on the highway for more. He was nabbed by a patrol car and failed the breath test.

"What's the matter with Kieran?" Alex asked Neil.

"He hasn't seen you for a while and he'd like to," Eileen said. "Only you. He doesn't want to see your father."

"Dad didn't cope well, after Kieran left," Alex said. "He was drinking too much."

"A problem we Piggott men have got to watch," Neil said.

"He and Mum were fighting. All the time. Over little things. And some big ones too. Then he lost his licence."

"So that's what happened. He never told me. I just heard he was moving out for a while so they could sort things out."

"Kieran thought of contacting your mum, then," Eileen said. "He wanted to see her. He should have seen her. But he didn't because he felt she'd have had enough to cope with, separating from your father. He didn't want to add to her burden. And he asked us not to tell. We keep our word."

"It's been hard," Neil said. "Trying to do the best for Kieran. Not knowing what was going on with Robert and your mother. I wondered whether the fight with Kieran was having an effect on Robert. The first story he told us, that Kieran had gone overseas, we knew was a fabrication. After all, we knew where Kieran was. And Kieran was coming out to see us every couple of weeks. Of course, as time went on and the story changed a bit I wanted to tell Robert I knew it was all a charade. But it was better to go along with him. Let him work through things. But he hasn't, has he Alex?"

"He's much better now. The drink shrink has helped him. That's this counsellor he started going to after he lost his licence. And being away from Mum made him appreciate her more. He'd send her flowers and stuff. He started inviting her out for dinner. It was getting a bit gooey. I'd come home and they'd be necking on the couch. Like they were young people. I didn't know where to look."

"Some of us oldies haven't completely gone to seed, you know Alex." Eileen smiled at him.

"So where is Kieran?" Alex asked.

"He's in a hospice," Neil said. "We've been going to see him. We haven't since you came here. But we're going in tomorrow to have Christmas lunch with him. He'd like you to come, if you want."

"What's wrong with him."

"He's sick."

"What with?"

"He's just finished some medication for pneumonia," Eileen said. "He seems a lot better."

"He's got AIDS, hasn't he."

"Yes," said Neil. "Yes, he's got AIDS."

"How?"

"I don't think that's a very relevant question now," Eileen said. "I don't want to know how or why or anything like that. He's just sick. He was such a beautiful boy." Slow tears trickled down her cheeks. She reached for a paper serviette to wipe them away. "I'm sorry, Alex. It's been hard. We've been living with this for about six months. He's only got really sick in the last six weeks. Very fast, the doctors say. And now Kieran wants to give up all the drugs he's on. He says it's not worth it."

"He's being very brave, Alex. Braver than anyone I know. Facing the whole thing straight up. I've seen plenty of airmen more scared of less. Your brother has got guts. Lots of guts. I'm very proud of him."

Alex remembered Kieran coming home totally smashed after his HSC was over, his T-shirt ripped open, one Reebok lost, half a packet of Marlboro squashed into the back pocket of his jeans, not even able to walk. He'd been crawling up the driveway at 5.30 in the morning. No-one knew how he got there. But Alex had heard him and helped him through the sleeping house and into bed.

"What time did Kieran get home last night?" his father had asked at breakfast. "Must have been late."

"I didn't hear him," his mother had said, "but I just put my head round his door. His room smells like brewery, so I think he'll have a bit of a sore head."

His father laughed: "Boys will be boys."

And he remembered that dinner for his mother's birthday. Kieran, seated at the table, announcing he had something to say. Everybody turned to him, as they always did, expecting a eulogy for his mother, some of his cleverness and wit. But instead he had stammered out that it was really difficult to be able to say this, he was proud to be gay, and he hoped they would accept him for what he was. The dinner was never finished, the food forgotten as the family digested instead Kieran's words. Robert had reacted by telling Kieran to stop with all that nonsense.

"It's not nonsense," Kieran had persisted.

His father drained his glass of wine and banged the glass down. "Don't be stupid," he told his son. I don't know where you've got this idea from, but it's extremely poor taste on your mother's birthday."

"I had to tell you. I don't want to live a secret life."

His father had moved to the liquor cabinet and poured himself a large scotch. He took a large mouthful. "I don't want to hit you, Kieran. I've tried never to hit my children. But you are pushing me to a point where no-one would blame me if I belted you. Understand this, you cannot be what you say you are. I will not let you. You are my son and it is impossible for that to happen. You can talk about secret lives, but if what you say is true you are better off dead. You are a normal, healthy seventeen-year-old. A little mixed up, maybe." He stopped for another mouthful of scotch. "But don't you try telling me you're some swishy queen. Now apologise to everyone, especially your mother."

"I can't apologise for being what I am. I'm not ashamed."

"Robert!" his mother shouted as his father charged at Kieran with his fists raised. But Kieran stepped to one side in a self-defence move. His father, too angry and too drunk to quickly react, smashed his shins into the coffee table. He swore furiously.

The rest of the group sat in silence listening to Robert's curses. Their mother stood up and went over to her husband. She put her hands up to his face.

"Come and sit down, Robert. We've had enough fuss."

"Dad's right, Mum," Tracey had piped up. "Kieran has to apologise. Especially to you."

"I do think this is all a bit uncalled for," his mother told Kieran as she led Robert over to his armchair. "It is a very tasteless joke."

"It is not a joke Mum." Kieran had tears in his eyes now. "I'm serious."

Robert began to yell. Whatever it was he was trying to say was unintelligible. His wife tried to hush him, but he simply shouted more loudly. His wife sat by him, attempting to keep him in his seat, her face crumpling as she too began to weep. Then the rest of them joined in, like a pack of barking dogs. Tracey and Lisa had shouted, spitting out foul words at Kieran, telling him he was a selfish little shit, ruining a family gathering with his disgusting revelations.

"Go to bed, Alex," his mother had said at one point. "You are too young for this."

Alex had gone. But in his bedroom he had heard how they had hounded Kieran away. Their shouts and screams drove Kieran to his room, as well. Alex could make out him packing clothes and belongings through the curtains. Alex opened his door and watched his family keep up the barrage as Kieran brushed past them to the front door. Tracey had even thrown Kieran's Reeboks down the driveway as Kieran struggled his backpack into the taxi he'd managed to call, having to keep his hand cupped over the mouthpiece to keep the noise of the others from the operator.

"He totally messed things up, you know," Alex said. "Everything would have been alright if he'd just kept quiet about it."

"I don't think it was something he could keep quiet about," Neil answered. "He was trying to be honest to himself. Not pretend he was something he wasn't."

"But why was he like that? My own brother. We used to share the same bathroom."

"Does that mean you don't want to come with us when we go to see him tomorrow?" asked Eileen. "I'll have to leave Christmas lunch in the fridge for you then. You'll have to put it together yourself."

"No, I'll come with you," Alex said. "I'd like to see him. I've been wondering how he's getting on. I've kind of missed having him around."

"Well, let's get these tea things inside then," Neil said, "and get back to those seeds. We'll have to finish them today because there'll be no time tomorrow. And it looks like there'll be a storm this arvo." There were agitated, dirty clouds massing to the south.

"Before you have Alex do anything, dear, I'd like to give him the present from Kieran," Eileen said to Neil. "Come inside with me, Alex. It's in the linen cupboard."

Alex followed Eileen into the house. They walked out of sunshine into the sudden gloom of the hallway.

"I can't see till my eyes adjust," she said, "but it's on this shelf here. Can you reach in and get it?" Alex stretched over piles of fresh towels and pillowslips. His fingers touched a bulky paper shape. He pulled it out. It was a fat manilla envelope. His name was written on it in straggly black texta.

"If I were you," she told him, "I'd go to your room and open it. Don't worry about Neil. He'll manage the seeds. He did before you were here."

Alex went to his room, closed the door and sat on his bed. The manilla envelope had been sealed with sticky tape. He ripped the tape off and reached in. He pulled out a sheaf of lined writing paper and a big notebook. All of the sheets had been closely written on with a fine black artline pen. The top sheet was headed "read me first. Please read the sheets in order". He started:

Dear Alex
I'm sorry this is all I've got to offer you for Christmas. I wanted to get you something you'd like, but I couldn't. I'd been putting these together for some time, anyway, because I wanted to tell you about me.

I didn't even get to say goodbye last time I saw you. You'd been sent to your room. I told Dad I wanted to go and say goodbye to you. You were the only one who kept quiet. Even Mum was crying and saying "how could you?" over and over. Dad said there was no way I was going to taint you. Taint you! He's got a strange turn of phrase the old Dad. That'll be the lawyer in him. And the meanness that goes with that.

I don't forgive him.

I've tried, but I can't find it in me to do that.

Neil could take me in, though. Neil didn't judge me. Neil didn't think I'd taint anyone. He just asked what he could do to help. He said there would be some things he'd find difficult, but he'd see how he'd go. He never yelled at me and told me I had to leave the house because I was unclean, like Dad did. Neil said he'd help me do whatever I thought was best, even if I changed my mind later.

I don't know if I've changed my mind. I've changed, yes, but in the end I think I did the right thing. Neil said to me that night when I arrived at his place, "You can only do what you consider to be the right thing. It's important always to be true to yourself."

We'd gone out for a walk, and I was in a real bad way. Like I was a complete mess. I kept crying, and I felt superbad, and I just couldn't believe it. I was trying to tell Neil what I'd told everyone at home. It was hard. I expected him to react the same way as Dad did. That's because an old man like him would have to, being a digger and all that. And I had to be really clear what I was saying, because I didn't know if he'd even understand what being gay meant. He did, though. He was pretty cool about it. "Are you sure?" he asked me. "It won't be an easy life. I've never known one who was happy."

"I'm pretty sure," I said. "I know I'm different to other guys."

That was really my problem, Alex. For a long time I didn't realise I was not like everybody else. I thought everyone was like me. It seems stupid, I know, but the way I grew up I had never ever thought I was different. I didn't realise I loved boys because I didn't think about it. I was friends with lots of kids, girls and boys. I was part of a gang, and we all hung out together doing the same things, going to each other's parties, sitting next to each other at school. And, yes, I was always wanting to be with Steve Saker. You know how I always hung around with him. He was my special friend. But I didn't know I was in love with him. The way I felt about him was just something I grew into. It happened. It was always there and it felt good. It was good.

It's so crazy. I can't believe it now. How could I have been so innocent? So stupid! It's kind of nice to think I was, but it makes me feel a complete dumb-bum. It wasn't that I didn't know about sex and life and what goes on. I knew how men and women made love. I knew that was normal. I guess I thought I'd be doing that when I got married some time when I was much older. But the idea was just that. Something hypothetical. Something to do way off in the future. I was much keener to be with Steve. Maybe I thought I was going through a phase, if I ever thought about it at all. I don't know that I did. I never ever really consciously thought I was gay until Steve told me I was when we were in Year 11. That was how totally dumb and naive I was. He had to tell me, so I would stop harassing him. Which I was, because doing it with him was on my mind all the time. I'd always be trying to be alone with him. But he didn't want to be with me any more, because it had gone past just fooling around.

That Steve, he broke my heart but he opened my eyes.

It was like I had gone to sleep one night and woken up the next morning in another world. I was on a train in a tunnel with the lights out. And that last summer, when we were at Brewarrina with Grandma, I wanted to ask you did you mind but I couldn't find a way. I had crossed a line and gone from being one of the gang to being all alone. At first I was shocked. I couldn't be homosexual. I was perfectly normal. I didn't lisp, or flap my hands, or walk funny, or have long fingernails on my little pinkie, or want to wear women's clothing, or have an ear-ring. But I did lust after Steve. And when I thought about it there were other boys I would have liked to touch. The thrill I got in the change rooms after sport was much more exciting than when I looked at a *Playboy*.

Then there was Mr Bennett, our maths teacher that year. He was about twenty-five, I guess. He seemed a lot older to me. It's funny, now I'm closer to his age he seems a lot younger. But I haven't seen him since I left school. Before you get the wrong idea, he never did anything. It was all me, all in my mind. He was married with a little baby but I didn't let that stop me thinking about him, dreaming about his big lips kissing mine. Maths was never my strongest subject, but in Year 11, I zoomed ahead. I listened to Mr Bennett's every word. I stayed back after class to ask him about Euclid or Fibonacci. I sought him out in the staffroom to see whether he could give me extra problems to improve my performance in maths. I don't think he ever knew I was doing it all just to see him as often as I could. I certainly didn't think, consciously, any of that. Until Steve made me think about it.

So the rest of that year, and all of Year 12, I knew I was gay. I thought I must be sick or strange or something till I read about a group for young gay guys. I found out where they met and I went there. The first time I was too frightened to go in. The second time, I was going to go back to the station, too, but I saw these two guys going in who didn't look like they had two heads or anything, so I followed them in. It was great, because all of the people I met that night were as unsure of themselves as I was. And they were all pretty normal. I knew I wasn't such a freak after that.

I was really worried about you, Alex. I'd been looking out for you. I was trying to help you in ways where I hadn't had any. I could blame Dad for that. I used to. But it wasn't his fault that he didn't know how to be a father. It is his fault that he doesn't know how to be a human being, though! Anyway, I was trying for you. But once I knew I was different, I worried what I could do to you. I don't mean I'd have tried anything on. I guess I was thinking like Dad. I didn't want to taint you, which is why when he said that it hurt so much. Because you trusted me Alex, and I couldn't do the same for you.

I think now it would have been great to have been able to talk to you then about it when we had some time together. I couldn't talk to Dad. I knew that. But you were twelve, then. It wouldn't have been right, would it? What would you have thought? What do you think now? I don't know. I've been assuming you think differently from Dad. Maybe you don't. I never thought of that until now.

I've been so lucky with Neil and Eileen. They have helped me all along the way. It can't have been easy for them. It hasn't been easy for me, so anybody else will have had a bumpy ride. But I did it all because I thought it was the right thing. I keep coming back to that, don't I. The right thing. I still believe that. I do.

Would I do it any other way? I don't know another way. There was no road map for me to follow. I had to push through the dark tunnel, feeling my way. The darkness hides a lot of things that can bring harm. As well as a lot of things that are worth finding. I found good things, and some not so good, but I found my own way. I did that, Alex. It mightn't seem much to you. Your world has streetlights, and paths and roads for you to follow. You know where you are going. I didn't know where I was going, but I found out for myself. I'm proud of that.

I'm raving. The drugs do that. I'm stopping them.

I'd like to see you Alex. I hope you will want to see me. I miss you. Please come and visit me. Your brother,

Kieran.

Alex held the letter on his lap. He didn't try to read it again. The words had already singed themselves into his memory. He looked down at the other item his brother had given him. There was even more to read.

Alex put the letter back in the envelope and picked up the notebook. It had a black cover with a red spine. Roughly blocked gold printing on the back declared it to be a product of the People's Republic of China. The cover was scuffed and had the outlines of various mugs and glasses staining it. In the top right corner, the name Kieran Piggott was neatly printed in silver ink. The pages were lined, and the ink on each page ranged from blue to red to green to black. Some passages were in pencil. Alex started at the beginning.

Wednesday 20 April 1988
I didn't want this to happen. I was only trying to tell mum and dad what I'd finally had the courage to admit to myself. Did dad think I was so pleased about it? I'd wished I could change. Why would I want to be so different to everyone else? I've tried to think like a straight, but it doesn't work. Neil and Eileen have been so good. The $500 they have lent me will be great. The room I looked at today will be okay for a while. I wonder what it'll be like living with other gay people? That Maurice guy was really over the top! He sure wears a lot of make-up. Real stereotype, like they say at Young Gays. That was a good idea of the group, for us all to start a journal and write down things that happen to help us deal with them. Don't think I'll share this with anyone there yet, though. Not till I

feel comfortable with them all. Wouldn't want them judging me on this sort of stuff. It'd stop me writing what I feel. Am I supposed to like Maurice just because he's gay? I don't want to wear make-up, and his bangles were horrible. And he had bad breath. But I like the look of that guy Phillip. He reminds me a lot of Steve. Which is probably not a good thing. I should try to find someone I like who doesn't remind me of Steve. If I pay Neil and Eileen back at $5 per week it will take 100 weeks. That's nearly two years! I'll have to do it faster than that. Got to get a job. Mission: Get a job! How to do it: Hell, I don't know. I'm only a seventeen year old faggot first time in the city! Maybe I should try at the CES.

Monday 25 April 1988
Anzac Day. All the old diggers marching. I went up to Mt Kuring-gai to see Neil and Eileen and thank them for helping me move into my new place. Crown Street is full of people all the time. It's fantastic to be so close to all the action. But it is noisy and dirty. I asked Neil how come he doesn't march, seeing how he's got such a famous medal and everything. He said he has his own private dawn service by himself. There's a uniform night at the Shift tonight to celebrate Anzac Day. I'm going with Maurice and Hugh. Maurice wanted to go as a WRAN, but we talked him into something a bit more butch. He's actually all right if he remembers to clean his teeth. He's got awful cold sores though. Hugh says Maurice has spent too many years down on his knees in the dark. I think Maurice is really old. Over thirty. He talks about the good old days. He was telling me there used to be lots of clubs where you just went and fucked. There are not so many of them now. I don't know if I'd like them. But they've all closed down since the epidemic. Too many of the older guys got the virus in places like that. Maurice has lost so many friends. Hugh has lent me some pants and a cap so I can go as a U.S. Marine. He's going as a sailor. They said I should go as something Australian seeing it's the Bicentennial, but I couldn't think of anything Australian that was sexy enough.

Sunday 1 May 1988
I got a job yesterday! It's horrible, but it's money. I start Tuesday. At 5.30. And I don't finish till 12. Dishwashing! And cleaning. And running around doing what nobody else wants to do. But there's a chance I could work up to be a waiter. And it's $5 an hour. So I'll get nearly $200 a week! I've got to get something for Alex for his birthday next month, and pay back Neil, and pay the rent. Will I have any money left?

Tuesday 17 May 1988
This cool guy has asked me out. Except I can only go on Monday when I don't work. Work sure cuts down your social life. He's old. About 30, I think, but he doesn't look it. He's really good-looking. He's got a Celica. I met him at the Shift after work last night. He wanted me to go back to his place. We just had a cup of coffee instead. He's going to pick me up at 7 and we're going to go out to dinner. I feel really nervous. He wears Paco Rabanne aftershave. I like that one a lot. It's very expensive.

Tuesday 24 May 1988
Brian took me to dinner at Taylor's in Surry Hills. He paid. It cost a fortune. It was strange. We had sausages, and little chickens. There was lemon ice: sorbet I think. One price covered everything. Four courses, all one after the other. With red wine. It was in the courtyard, with lots of little lights. Kind of romantic. Especially with Brian to look at. We had liqueurs after. I got a bit pissed. Then Brian drove us back to his place and I spent the night with him. He's a bit rough in bed. I don't know if I want to keep seeing him if he wants to be like that all the time. I told him I was new to things and hadn't been fucked much before. He wouldn't stop when I asked him to. It still hurts. The water in the toilet was red after I did a shit. I asked Maurice if I should do anything. He said it was just my hymen breaking and that it'd go away. I hope it will. Brian really hurt me. I won't let him do it again.

Friday 3 June 1988
A day after my birthday. I got really bombed at the Shift last night. I nearly got chucked out. Don't know how I managed to stagger home. I didn't think it would be so hard to break up with Brian. I really like him but I hate the way he wants to have sex. I didn't like the way he tried to slip me a rohypnol. He'd have fucked me when I was unconscious. Oh well, here I am, 18 and on the scrap heap of life. No-one wants me. Unless I'm drugged unconscious. Says a lot for my warm, bright personality doesn't it. Poisonality more like it. Maurice isn't talking to me because I vomited on his Persian rug in the living room. But I will send Alex's birthday present off. He should have a good birthday. Maybe I should let him know I'm o.k. But I'm not o.k. am I?

Monday 4 July 1988
Why do people just want to fuck you? I hate older guys. They are users and cheats. I am sick of them all. I am sick of the Albury, and the Newtown, and the Oxford, and the Shift and Crown St and the whole

damn scene. Dad was right, dad was right. This is going to be a rotten, rotten life and I wish I could be someone else now now now!

Sunday 31 July 1988
This guy at Young Gays was making eyes at me. He is so cute. I thought he must have been keen on the guy next to me, but no, he was making eyes at me. He's got the nicest smile. His name is Arturo. I wonder where he's from? He speaks English without an accent, but he looks Spanish or something. Nice skin. Don't see him for another week. Maybe then I should ask him out for coffee. Or a drink. Or maybe just home to go to bed. He's got a really hot body. And brown eyes.

Wednesday 10 August 1988
Arturo asked me out for coffee! We had it at that weird cafe in Crown Street where the waiters are all trannies. He is Spanish! Or rather South American. His parents speak Spanish, and he can too. He spoke to me in Spanish. I asked him what he said, but he said he didn't want to translate it because I'd think he was just trying to get into my pants. I think he said something like he'd like to fuck with me. Well, I'd like to do it with him. If I didn't have work, I think we'd have done it yesterday. I said to him he could get into my pants if I could get into his. It wasn't very clever, but I am meeting him for a drink tonight at 12.30 at the Shift. I can't wait!

Friday 12 August 1988
Yippee! Arturo and I did it. And did it and did it and did it and did it! It was fantastic! He is so good in bed, and he is such a nice person. His kisses are soft. And he doesn't try to push anything. He let me fuck him! Three times! And he fucked me. It was so good sleeping with him. And we made ourselves breakfast and ate it on his balcony. He shares a unit with a couple of guys who are living together, but they want him to move out soon so they can have more room. He said why don't we get somewhere together. I think it is too soon. No, I don't! I want to be with him all the time. But he doesn't have a job. He's on the dole. Maybe I could keep him chained up as a sex slave. I'd like that. But I think he'd soon get tired of it. I think I'm in love.

Monday 5 September 1988
We have our own little one-bedroom flat. It is dirty and daggy and it smells of old cooking and farts and smelly feet, and the carpet looks like a rubbish pit and it costs as much a week as I earn and we have to get a fridge and furniture and a telephone, but we have a mattress and we are

sleeping together all the time and it is super-fan-bloody-tastic Arturo stop reading over my shoulder I said this was private.

Monday 10 October 1988
Arturo has a job, Arturo has a job! He has got a position as a sales assistant at Boys Plus. He can get clothes from there at a discount. And he gets paid more than me. We're rich, we're rich! Well, not that rich, but yesterday I went up to Mt Kuring-gai and paid Neil the last of the money I owed him. And I'm going to get training to be a waiter, which will mean more money and better work and Arturo is rubbing his dick in my hair to make me stop writing.

Thursday 17 November 1988
I gave Arturo his birthday present. He was very pleased with it. It was so hard to keep it secret from him. Sal and Ramona are coming over on Saturday and we'll go out and have lunch before I have to go to work. But next week I get two nights a week off. Arturo and I are going up to Mt Kuring-gai together on Sunday. I told Eileen it was his birthday, so she said come and have lunch. Two lunches out this weekend. We'll end up porky little ten-tonnes. I will have to work it off Arturo when I come home tonight. No not now Arturo the girls will be here soon and they won't want to find us in bed fucking. Or up against the door. You are really dirty-minded, but I guess that's why I love you so much.

Sunday 20 November 1988
Arturo liked Eileen and Neil. I am not sure they were so keen on him. There were a lot of silences. I felt uncomfortable too. Neil told a joke about fairies. I know he was just trying to be himself, but his jokes aren't funny even when they aren't about fairies.

Christmas Day 1988
Hope Alex likes his present. Arturo and I went to Neil and Eileen's in the afternoon. The train was so slow. They had been over to Mum and Dad's for lunch. Neil said dad was drunk and noisy, but Alex was fine. No sign of the CD I sent him. But I don't think Neil or Eileen would recognise Jimi Hendrix. Alex will like the guitar work. Now that I have discovered Hendrix I am going to buy all his recordings. He is great. Arturo's Mum sent us a card. No news from his Dad though. Arturo saw her last week and she'd been beaten up again. I'm so tired!

Saturday 28 January 1989
We have been together for over three months.

Tuesday 14 February 1989
Valentine's Day. Arturo gave me some incredibly stupid underwear. A red heart g-string, and a pair of briefs with "Hands off my baby" on them. I gave him some edible undies from the Toolshed. He put them on. I ate them off but they tasted like horrible chewing gum. They made a mess of his pubes.

Sunday 5 March 1989
Mardi Gras is over. And we are both pooped! Too much raging, too much dancing and too much fun! Arturo had the bright idea of us dressing as Olympic swimmers. It was an easy costume. Just swimmers. But where do you put a wallet in swimmers? We ended up walking around with money stashed down the front of our swimmers and having to dig a hand down to grab it whenever we needed a drink or had to pay for anything. We stayed in the swimmers all night, and I had to pry all these hands and eyes off Arturo. He certainly looked hot. And I didn't think I looked too bad either. Neither did a few other hot guys, which started Arturo off. He was sulking for hours. The party was great. We had scored some ecstasy from the girls. We were peaking when we arrived. Then this great looking guy in leather kept giving us amyl. He wanted us to go off with him. I was tempted but Arturo talked me out of it. "He's a leather queen," he said. "All of them have AIDS." But he still had great pecs.

Thursday 20 April 1989
A year since I started this journal. Neither Arturo or I have kept going to Young Gays. We don't need to now we have each other. So this is only for him and me. And we have been living together over six months. When I come home from work, like now, he is already cuddled up in bed asleep. Sometimes he holds a pillow, and hugs it. Other times his head is resting on his hands and he's snuggled up on his side. He likes the left hand side and I like the right. His side is closest to the clock, because he needs that in the morning. My side is furthest away from the window so the light doesn't wake me up too early. His brown shoulders are peeping out from the top of the sheet. I really want to get into bed beside him and start fucking. But he has to start early, so if I do he'll only be cross at me. He is so cute. He has really changed my life.

Wednesday 26 April 1989
So we have had Anzac Day again. I feel straaannngggeee! We took speed last night. It was very cool. We didn't need to have anything to drink. We stayed high all night, dancing and having a fantastic time. Arturo is such a

rager when he's high. He wanted to fuck everywhere we went, in the toilets, in corners, everywhere. It was just as well we couldn't get it up too often, or we might have been arrested. We nearly got chucked out of DCM because he was trying to suck me off under a table. It was so funny. And when we came home we couldn't get to sleep so we went off to Bronte and did an early morning walk around the cliffs past Tamarama to Bondi. The sun was just up and the sea looked superb! The best thing I have ever seen. The sea was smooth. Like glass, with the sun riding on it like some solid golden sheet. And there was hardly anybody about. Some surfers catching early morning waves. We perved at them. There was a jogger or two, but everybody else was still in bed. Where we ended up having a super long fuck with Arturo as horny as anything wanting to fuck me and be fucked and just everything. I don't know how I'm going to get through my shift. I am exhausted and my head is going bzzz bzzz bzzz. I like speed. We'll have to try it again. Only thing I don't like is the needle. But Arturo can do it for me. Right Arturo? I know you'll read this when you wake up. And you better go to work tomorrow, because that old queen you work for was pretty put out when I rang to tell him you were too sick to come in. I don't think he was fooled.

Monday 3 May, 1989

We are going to a party at these guys' place in Newtown. We met them at Mardi Gras. We have seen them a few times around the place and we like them. They are both older. They want to have us come over and get friendlier. I know what they want to do. They really liked our Mardi Gras costumes. I don't know what will happen but we are looking forward to going. They own their own house. How can they be that rich already? Nick is a schoolteacher and Steven is a pharmacist. Which is the good part. He knows what drugs are really good. He has promised he'll have speed for all of us, and coke. And it's all part of the party. There's going to be just six of us. It might turn into an orgy! I don't know what I'll do. "Remember the condoms," Arturo keeps saying. We haven't been using them ourselves because we're both too young to have picked up the virus and they kept breaking when we were fucking. When Arturo is on speed and fucking he just goes and goes for hours. It's fantastic. I can't believe I never used to like being fucked and that it hurt. It never hurts with Arturo. In fact, when he's pounding away is when I like it best. Maybe I shouldn't let him know that. Too late!

Sunday 9 May 1989

What a night at Nick and Steven's! When we arrived they had their friends Jean-Claude and Walter there. Jean-Claude is French. He is very attractive, and such a slut. He started taking his clothes off after he'd had a glass or two of champagne. Then he was sitting in everyone's lap, kissing and trying to take clothes off. Steve had some speed which we all took so we were all a little off our tits. Arturo and Jean-Claude were really getting into tongue kissing each other, Jean-Claude was completely naked, and he took Arturo's shirt off. Then we all started to hug the two of them, and to take our clothes off. Jean-Claude and Arturo were sixty-nining on the floor. Steven and Walter had a dildo. They started to put it up Jean-Claude's arse. It was a really big one. I didn't think anything that big could fit. But they got it up. Nick and I were kissing and watching. Then Nick wanted to fuck me. I said he had to wear condoms, which he did, but watching the others really got him going. He fucked me good and slow and hard. Arturo was watching us and when Nick had finished he had me move so I was sucking Jean-Claude and Arturo was fucking me. He wanted to use the dildo too, but Steven said it would need a good wash before it could be used on someone else. Nick came out with another one and Arturo pulled out and put that up me and then fucked me again. He kept alternating. Then he asked Nick and Steven to put the dildo he and I were using up his arse while he fucked me. Jean-Claude was fucking Walter. His arse was right in front of my face so I could stick out my tongue and lick it as he thumped in and out of Walter. Steven had this great amyl. The rush was fantastic and Arturo came. But he was so hot he wanted to be fucked. I fucked him until I came. It was really great because Steven held the dildo up me the whole time. The feeling with the amyl was just sensational. Then Nick, and Walter, and Steven fucked Arturo one after the other. He wanted them to. He was really into being fucked. They were doing this in the kitchen, where Arturo could bend over a counter so I could kiss him and hug him. Jean-Claude was playing with Arturo's cock and balls. I made sure the other guys all wore condoms. When they were all finished Arturo's arse was wet, and soft, and I could almost put my whole hand in it. But he was really out of it so I put him to bed in Nick and Steven's spare bedroom. It was about five in the morning by then. We had been fucking almost all night. It was really out of this world. Nick made us champagne and orange juice as the sun came up. I went to the spare room with Arturo. The speed wouldn't let me drop off to sleep. I was buzzing. And then I got an erection that wouldn't go away. So I rolled Arturo where I could get at him, and I slipped up him. He didn't wake up or anything. His arse was so loose and slippery and warm, though. I stayed up him for hours, and then finally shot. What do you think, Arturo?

Saturday 27 May 1989

We went up to see Neil and Eileen again. It was much better this time. Everybody was more relaxed. But Arturo did say "We went to this really good party a couple of weeks ago". I thought he was going to start telling them about it. But Arturo just said it was in Newtown. Apparently Neil had been saying he used to live near there, in Enmore. I'd missed that because I was helping Eileen carry out some plates. Maurice died yesterday. The funeral is on Monday. I haven't been to one before.

Saturday 3 June 1989
Arturo organised a great night for my birthday. We ended up dancing most of it at DCM and the Shift. He had got some eccy from Steven. And, since the night we were over at Nick and Steven's, Arturo and I are having such mind-blowingly good sex. I wondered at first if it would ruin things, us having sex with other people. But it hasn't. We have found it just makes the sex we have together even better because we have found out things we both like to do. I really like to screw Arturo. I did it to him every which way. He wanted me to. I fucked him and fucked him, and he kept groaning "I love you, I love you".

Thursday 22 June 1989
I got a pay rise, without even asking! An extra two dollars an hour. Maybe because I let them know I'm nineteen now. But I don't think I want to work there too much longer. Even with the extra money the work is too hard. I'm going to try one of the big hotels. I'd like to work at the InterContinental and their hotel school. That would give me good training. I know a guy who's a waiter in the Treasury Restaurant there and he has given me the name of the woman to call about a job. It would mean I would have to change shifts around, but I would get more experience. I have found out from TAFE too where I can do a hospitality course so I could enrol in that next year if I can't get into one of the hotels.

Tuesday 4 July 1989
American Independence Day. So we had to do American things. We had hot dogs for dinner. And now I feel sick because they were full of spicy junk. I keep burping up the taste. Arturo is farting in the bed really bad so the place smells. I had to get up and breathe some fresh air. Peeyoo! He has done it again. Arturo, I am going to make you pay for this in the morning!

Thursday 13 July 1989

This customer at work last night tried to pick me up. He said he would like to see me again, privately, and gave me his card. He is a barrister. But he's about thirty-five. He had on a very attractive suit and a nice tie. I would never be able to afford a tie like that. He had three guests for dinner and he paid for them all, in cash, no trouble. His guests weren't gay, and I don't think they knew he was, because he spoke to me out near the kitchen where no-one could see. "This is my private number," he said, pointing at one of the four on the card. "Call me there and it'll be our secret." I think he's a bit creepy. And how could he pick me when I was working? I don't look any different to any of the other guys. I don't think I'll call him.

Tuesday 1 August 1989
I went to see the woman at the InterContinental this afternoon. She was very impressed with my HSC results and my experience. She said they didn't have anything at the moment but positions came up all the time and she would put me on file. She said they would help with a TAFE course by trying to leave my shifts so they didn't interfere with classes and they would give me time off for exams and things. That is something. Good! She said there was a lot of competition for their hotel school though.

Saturday 5 August 1989
Wet weather. I got drenched coming home. I had forgotten my umbrella. And the heater gave up the ghost. It blew up! Flash bang! I thought I would have to replace a fuse, which I didn't know how to do, but all that I had to do was turn the switch back on. I don't understand electricity. Arturo was really late home. Now that he is training to be a hairdresser they are making him work really hard for peanuts, so we don't have much money. He had to sweep the floor and wash heads and fold heaps of alfoil for his boss. She is such a bitch. She tells him: "You'll never make a good hairdresser if you don't listen to me. You've got to put in the hours now, or you'll never be able to cut properly." And she puts him down in front of the other staff and the customers. I don't know how he can bear it. But he says the ladies who come to the salon are alright, and they talk to him nicely and tell him not to worry about Michelle, it's probably just her time of the month. But she's like that all the time. He's so tired he's already gone to bed.

Saturday 24 August 1989
We have to move. This really shits me. The rent has been put up far too high. The place was sold a couple of months ago, and the new owner wants new tenants. So the rent goes up and we have to move! I wish we

could get enough money together so we could buy a place. It would be so much better than paying rent and getting kicked out and having to move. I want to shift further down into Surry Hills. Somewhere like Fitzroy St, or Collins St. Or I wouldn't mind Elizabeth Bay. Arturo wants to stay in Darlinghurst. But the one place our agent had to show was a pigsty compared to our present nice little unit. It was in an old building full of junkies. Too many of them. We'd be burgled every other day.

Tuesday 3 September 1989
Two days in our new place. It doesn't have much light. I thought it would get to us. And the ventilation seems bad. It is only the beginning of spring but Arturo sweated all night. He was dripping wet. I have had to air the sheets, but this place has no good spots to hang things out. I've slung the sheets across the living room and Arturo will have to make the bed when he comes home. Another funeral tomorrow. Arturo's old boss at Boys Plus. To think he was always trying to get Arturo to have it off with him! Just as well. He never looked sick at all. He took pills. I never liked him, but Arturo feels we should go out of respect. These old guys are such sleazebags.

Wednesday 13 September 1989
Last night was the first one Arturo has made it through without getting too hot. The humidity in this place is really bad. It is affecting me, too. We both wake up drenched. Today I will go to Grace Bros and buy a fan. Actually, I think I will try Target. They will be cheaper. I wish we could afford an air conditioner. Nick and Steve have a fully ducted system throughout their house. I have been saving some money, but the fan will take care of most of it.

Saturday 21 October 1989
I met Arturo at the Shift after work last night. He had gone to drinks with the girls after he had finished at the salon and he was a bit smashed. I didn't want to stay out late but he did. I was with him till almost 2, then I went home. Not straight home. I stopped at Numbers on the way and watched some movies. A couple of guys tried to grope me but I wasn't in the mood. I had to get up and let Arturo in when he finally got home because he was too pissed to be able to put the key in the lock.

Saturday 18 November 1989
I took Arturo out to dinner for his birthday last night, and to the movies. We had a really nice evening with just the two of us. I really enjoy being with him and it's so good when we can have some time together like that.

It was a shame that in the middle of the movie he had a gastro attack. I don't think it was the food we had. We went to Dixon St and had Chinese. I had exactly the same as him, because we shared dishes, and I wasn't sick. He missed about twenty minutes of "Batman" which he had been really wanting to see.

Christmas Day 1989
We had our own little Christmas together today. Both of us enjoyed being able to sleep in. We had coffee and croissants, then we took a picnic to the Botanic Gardens. We drank champagne and orange juice. Two bottles of champagne! After we had eaten, we took our shirts off and lay on our blanket in the sun. We both got a little burned, but we won't peel. Arturo has gone down to see his mother for Christmas dinner. I feel quite lonely. I thought of ringing home and maybe talking to Alex, but Dad would probably answer the phone. I tried to call Neil and Eileen, but they are still out. I got them some nice prints for Christmas. Botanical ones. I sent Alex two CDs. There is nothing on television. I hope Arturo won't be too late home.

Tuesday 2 January 1990
My head still hurts! We spent New Year's Eve at a party at Edgecliff. This guy called Sean who Nick and Steven know has a flat there with a balcony that gave us a view of the fireworks. The fireworks were great. But I drank too many champagne cocktails. Nick and Steven say Sean stars in porno movies and they are going to show us one.

Thursday 8 February 1990
I have bought myself a leather jacket. I've always wanted one. It cost me $450, but at least it is all paid for, not like Arturo's shoes! I have been wearing it ever since I got it. It feels really sexy. I'll wear it to work, but I'll have to get a padlock for my locker or someone will steal it. It smells terrific. But it is hot.

Friday 16 March 1990
We went over to Nick and Steven's last night and had dinner up on King Street then went back and watched this movie with Sean in it. "Take my big dick, man. Take it, you know you want it." "Give me some of your big cock. I really want your big cock." The lines are very funny when you've met the person who is saying them. And he was putting on this American accent. Arturo keeps coming out of the bathroom saying "Take my big dick, man" but he can't stop laughing, so it is just really stupid. I didn't realise Sean had such a good body.

Saturday 21 April 1990
I have passed my first hotel school exams. Now I have been allocated better shifts, and I can change around a lot more. It's great not to be fixed to one routine.

Thursday 10 May 1990
The night before last, the hot water in the flat above ours broke. We woke up to hear water dripping through our ceiling. It was a complete mess, and the agents wouldn't do anything. But finally I've forced them to fix it. Agents are such slimes. Now we just have to clean up. The plumbers made a big mess and carried on about poofs and AIDS. Bloody rude pigs!

Saturday 2 June 1990
My birthday. Arturo cooked me breakfast and then fed it to me after he had tied my hands up. He spooned stuff into my mouth. It was gross, but a real turn-on. He ended up feeding me something else, and we had wild sex, me still with my hands tied. A great birthday present.

Tuesday 10 July 1990
We have been thinking of having an overseas holiday. I went to a travel agent and got some brochures. I liked the thought of Bali, and Arturo thought Thailand sounded good. Especially as it is so cold out now. I am glad I have my leather jacket. It keeps me very warm. But we would need about $3000 just for a week in Bali. It is far too much. We can't afford it. Another winter in Darlinghurst, I guess.

Friday 17 August 1990
The streets are getting really dangerous. I got chased by these three Islander guys. Really big blokes. Scary. But I managed to outrun them. I reckon they wanted my leather jacket. Why can't they buy their own. I'm still shaking. I wanted to go out for a drink, but I'm too frightened. I'll have to wait until Arturo gets home.
Friday 7 September 1990
I started holidays today. I had a morning shift so I had finished work by 3, and now I have a whole week off! Arturo is furious that I am taking holidays while he still has to work but I had to do it. I have been getting so tired with the different shifts. I need some time to sleep in. And to see movies, and just relax. I'm going to go up to Mt Kuring-gai tomorrow, because Arturo is working, so then we can have Sunday. But I am going out raging tonight!

Sunday 20 October 1990
The flat stinks of smoke. The girls came over last night with some dope which we smoked and then Arturo started having a cigarette. Then another. The place reeks of cigarettes. If he takes up smoking full time he is going to have to get air freshener and clean out the ashtrays. But he hasn't even woken up yet!

Tuesday 13 November 1990
We are going to go away for Christmas. Nick and Steven have rented a house down the South Coast at Huskisson! They've invited us to come with them. All we have to do is find half the rent, which is $750 a week. Phew! But it will be for 10 days from Christmas Eve so we will have New Year down there too! Nick will drive us as well. It will be great. Steven is organising some super speed. And possibly some acid for New Year. We are going to have a fabulous time.

Thursday 27 December 1990
We have had a wonderful Christmas. Steven and I cooked the Christmas dinner. We didn't do anything traditional. We had chicken satay, and fresh prawns we bought green on Christmas Eve and cooked up, and a toffee cake, and potato salad. Steven is a good cook. He has taught me how to cook things properly. And we all slept together on mattresses on the floor. It was really nice. I could do this all the time.

Sunday 6 January 1991
It doesn't seem like New Year has come and gone. Back at work, grinding away. Arturo has finally left the bitch Michelle. He has found another place in Double Bay which will take him on as an apprentice. They won't pay him any more, but he will be better off not having to listen to that old bag. He pinched a pair of her cutters. They cost nearly $100, so he is saving himself some money. And she really owes him a lot more.

Friday 15 February 1991
Arturo stayed out all night. He had called me at work to say he would be late home because he was going to a Bobby Goldsmith benefit. He's gone before, and been home not long after me. I didn't think anything about it when I came home. I was so tired. It had been a really long night. We had a party booking. Though I did get a big tip. Usually when he's late home he snuggles up next to me, and I wake up and give him a kiss, and then we sleep. But I didn't wake up until six a.m. and he wasn't there. I worried he'd been bashed or something. I got up and got dressed because I thought I'd have to go and ask the police or whatever. I was just about to go out when he came in. He had gone off with someone. I was really

angry. I couldn't believe he'd just gone off with some stranger he'd met. He said it wasn't a stranger. He'd met this guy lots of times at different places. He said he wouldn't have gone with him if I'd been there, but he was feeling lonely and randy and the guy was hot so he just did what came naturally. I'm still very upset about it. I know we've never agreed to be totally faithful to each other, but this has really hurt me.

Saturday 2 March 1991
Arturo and I are not talking. Please talk to me Arturo. I know you read this. It is silly to ignore me. Anyway, I am taking your cigarettes because you owe me a packet.

Monday 4 March 1991
I met an American out here for Mardi Gras. At the Den. I went there after work. We started doing stuff at the Den and later went back to his hotel. He was staying at the Hyatt Kingsgate. I wanted Arturo to feel bad, but I was the one who did. Well, I think Arturo did, too, when I told him, but I felt sleazy and dirty doing it with this guy. He was o.k. but he kept telling me how beautiful I was and what a great body I had. Then he wanted to fist me. I didn't let him. Arturo said he really missed me and we went and had a nice brunch, and then walked in the Botanic Gardens. I don't like it when the two of us have these funny feelings between us. Are we even now Arturo? If we are going to go off with other people, can we talk about it first or only do it together? I don't want to own you. I just want us to be good for each other.

Friday 5 April 1991
We had a dinner out last night where we didn't argue. This was the first time in ages. Then we came home and went to bed. We just slept. We didn't do anything. But we did cuddle. Maybe we don't like each other sexually any more. I'm sure I still like Arturo. Just being near him makes me hard. I really enjoy fucking him, especially when he just relaxes and lets me. But he doesn't seem to want to do anything like that as often as we used to. He says it feels strange. I told him he should go and have it checked out. I hope I haven't hurt him somehow.

Wednesday 15 May 1991
I got home and Arturo was here. I wasn't expecting it, because he doesn't finish until 6.30. But he had been sick at work. He was very hot. I made him go to bed. He had been sitting up watching television. He's sleeping now. If he gives me flu I will be really pissed off. It has been going

around the hotel, and I have managed to avoid it so far. I have been eating lots of oranges and taking vitamin C.

Thursday 20 June 1991
The winter bugs have finally gone. My cold has cleared and Arturo is breathing like a normal person again instead of like some skulking monster. Tomorrow, I want to go and see a movie seeing as we can both sit without sniffling or coughing.

Saturday 27 July 1991
I made what I thought was a very nice dinner last night. Arturo has been feeling a bit sick for a few days, but this morning he said he was fine, so I thought I'd make something which would make him feel good. It wasn't much. Rice, salad and chicken curry. But the curry was very good, with basil leaves, and potatoes. I had spent an hour making the paste. Arturo took two mouthfuls, then he said he was going to be sick. He was on the toilet for ages. It was so smelly. He ruined the dinner. You did, Arturo. You could have not eaten whatever it was that stank so much. I hate it when he tells me to get fucked. My curry would have been much better for him. He only had two mouthfuls, so it can't have caused him to get the shits. He has been in such a lousy mood lately.

Saturday 24 August 1991
Arturo has lost his job. He has had to take so much time off because he's had this flu hanging around. He finally agreed he ought to go and see a doctor because it is hurting him if I try to fuck him. But there is nothing wrong with me. No discharge or anything. And there shouldn't be either. I hope I haven't hurt him somehow. I don't mean to be too rough, but I do like riding him. I shall try to hold myself back. But he hasn't actually arranged an appointment yet. He's a bit embarrassed, which I can understand. I will try and go with him to that practice in Taylor Square. At least they advertise in the *Star Observer* so they should understand us a bit. Maybe I have ripped him somehow. I hope he goes soon so we can get back to doing what we enjoy.

Thursday 12 September 1991
I have just brought Arturo back from the doctor. They wanted us both to go in. The test results were back. They told him he is HIV positive. The clinic wants me to go in for a test tomorrow. I don't understand. The only times we haven't had safe sex have been with each other. He has some skin things, and problems with his lungs. And a big infection in his bum. Some T-cell thing too. This shouldn't be happening to us. We're not supposed to get AIDS. We're too young.

Thursday 19 September 1991
Me too.

Thursday 17 October 1991
We have started some counselling and have been given all these guidelines on what we should do. Arturo doesn't care about them. I have tried to go through them with him but he says what's the use. We have been having joint counselling but I think I will ask if I can go by myself. Arturo says nothing in the sessions.

Saturday 9 November 1991
We are back having joint sessions. I asked if I could go by myself and the counsellor said it was up to me. But Arturo went ape after I told him I had been to a session by myself. He said I was deserting him and didn't care about him any more now that I had infected him. I suggested we ought to talk about that with the counsellor. He started crying and shut himself in the bathroom. I can't believe any of this is happening. I feel alright, but I wonder what is happening inside me. I had a dream the other night that my blood had worms in it and they were eating me from inside. I told the counsellor when we went there again yesterday. He said nothing. Nor did Arturo again.

Friday 13 December 1991
Arturo has come back. I told him it was no use going back to his mother's. He was there three days. He said he hated it. I told him I thought he hated me. He said he hated everything. I said I didn't think that was a very positive approach. He said fuck off. I was going to go out, but then he said he was sorry and not to leave him he was feeling so bad he needed me. Please give me a hug, he said, I haven't had one for ages. So I did.

Christmas Day 1991
We didn't go up to Mt Kuring-gai. I called in the morning and spoke to Neil and Eileen and wished them the best. They had invited us, but we said we had another invitation. They were going to have a quiet lunch. Dad hasn't asked them to Turramurra this year. In the afternoon we went over to Sal and Ramona's. They had organised a big Christmas party for orphans. We stayed until about six. The party was really raging by then, but we just weren't in the mood. I gave Arturo a Discman for Christmas. He said I needn't have bothered. I have already given him more than enough. He didn't even open it. He didn't give me anything.

Friday 3 January 1992
Arturo didn't want to do anything for New Year. Then late on New Year's Eve he did. He wanted to go out partying and dancing. We went up to Oxford St but we hadn't organised any tickets for any of the parties so we couldn't get in anywhere. We had been invited over to Nick and Steven's. Arturo didn't want to go there until we found nothing else was available. So we grabbed a taxi and went to Newtown. The party there was pretty good. We didn't arrive until about 11 and we stayed until 6. Arturo wanted to drink and smoke everything in sight. He ended up passing out. I left him for a couple of hours, then managed to get him into a taxi. When we got home we both crashed and slept right through until the next day, spooned up against each other even though it was too hot. I loved being able to hold him close for so long.
Thursday 6 February 1992
Arturo was really sick last night and I had to take him to the hospital. Once they knew he was sick with the virus they took him straight to the ward they have there. He had to go on a ventilator. Then they were shooting him with drugs. I waited for a while, then a nurse told me he'd have to stay over. He should be able to come home tomorrow.

Saturday 7 March 1992
Mardi Gras night and we are sitting at home listening to music and reading. Neither of us wanted to go out. We sent out for pizzas. Of course it took ages for them to be delivered because there were so many people in the streets. I tried to argue for a discount, but the delivery guy said we were lucky to get any at all. We are drinking scotch and Coke. Arturo keeps falling asleep.

Monday 14 April 1992
I went to the hospital to see Arturo. He will be able to come home on Thursday. There were two guys sitting on a bench near me. They were hardly saying anything, just sitting smoking. I don't know what they were there for. Then one says to the other, out of the blue, "How's your love life?" "I'm seeing someone at the moment. It's good," is the reply. "Sounds like it could be getting serious." "Ah, it's just a rooting relationship." I could do with a rooting relationship.

Saturday 23 May 1992
I went out last night. I couldn't stand being in the flat. Arturo is sleeping all the time. He was okay about me doing it. I don't think he knew whether I was there or not. I went to the Den. I wanted sex. That's all I

wanted. Just something in the dark. This guy tried to kiss me, but I didn't want that. I wanted him down there, down on his knees. He got down and I made him suck me. He did it for about half an hour before he got sick of it. I stayed in the dark, waiting. Another guy came along. He wanted me to fuck him. I put on a condom and fucked him for ages until he came. He still wanted me to do it, but I didn't want to unless his dick was stiff. I was still hard. He said he'd suck me. He went down on me, and then to my balls. "Turn around," he told me. He wanted to lick my arse. I thought, no, that can make you sick. But then I thought, so what. He passed me a bottle of amyl and I turned around and sniffed it and let him put his tongue where he wanted it. That got him really hot and stiff again, so I fucked him again, and finally came. I went home and Arturo was snoring. The drugs are doing that to him. I lay awake next to him, listening, for hours. When I did drift off it was only for a few minutes at a time.

Tuesday 2 June 1992
Twenty-two today. Hurray. What more can I say? Neil and Eileen sent me a card and a cheque. I shall have to tell them soon. I am going to get a cake and take it to Arturo. He probably won't want any, but the nurse there will offer it around to the other guys.

Friday 17 July 1992
I went up to Mt Kuring-gai early. Neil and Eileen were going shopping in Hornsby. I went with them. We parked in the Northgate car park. It was crowded out. Neil did his block finding a space. I helped them do all the grocery shopping at Safeway. After that, they wanted to get some things in Grace Bros so I wheeled the shopping trolley out to the car. A woman saw me and stopped behind me with her blinker on. She figured I was going soon and she could have our space. I ignored her, and just put all the groceries in the car. When I'd finished I slammed the boot closed and turned around and gave the woman the finger. Then I went back inside. You should have seen her face when I gave it to her. It made my day. I told Neil and Eileen what was wrong with Arturo and me. They didn't say anything.

Thursday 20 August 1992
Alyson has got me some Valium. I have taken them. She is going to call Neil and Eileen to tell them. She has rung Arturo's mother and father.

Friday 21 August 1992

Arturo's parents came and took all his stuff from the flat. "Is this his?" his father asked. "Is this his?" That's all he said. His father even tried to take the fridge and stereo. I said we owned them together. He wants me to pay him for Arturo's half. His mother wouldn't look at me. She didn't say anything to me. She just packed Arturo's things into a suitcase as his father gave them to her. They are going to arrange the funeral. They didn't tell me where. They said it would be only family. "We don't want none of his funny friends," his father said. I noticed Arturo's mother has bruises again. Neil and Eileen have said I should go up to Mt Kuring-gai. I don't know what to do.

Tuesday 8 September 1992
Inside the crematorium the fires have been lit. But they are not burning for me. I am going to go into the ground. I am going to be buried in a non-believers' section. I could be cremated if I wanted to. But I want to be buried. I have settled it. Not many people have the chance to book their own funeral. How lucky I am! But I had to do it. It makes things seem right. I wish my Mum and Dad were here.

Wednesday 14 October 1992
There is a hard white heat. I can see only the burning glare in an arid Marrickville blue sky curiously clear of planes. The fierce midday light shimmers above the asphalt, bakes the bricks, desiccates the roses, and reflects the heat back up in palpable layers from the concrete. Here, in this little layer of air where life creates itself in the strange chemistry that sunlight wreaks, life gasps with the sheer burden of it all, but does not yet relinquish its tenuous hold. The sun will once again slowly pass across the sky. But right now, Marrickville waits out the heat. There are places of relief. Not all the world is asizzle. In a gym five blocks away, inflated boys grunt up weights, flex biceps, sweat, sip water and say "how many reps is that?" to the inflated boys next to them. There's been no peeking before this. But with a sip of water, the eyes of the boys unstick and flick, now pencil cameras sliding lenses over and into all the mitochondria and scleroderma respirating in front of them. "Hot eh", they say, and smile, and maybe the smile is an invitation, or a threat, or just a smile (and I wish I was one of them, doing it). But here at the hospice, two young men sit on a bench on the verandah which runs down left of the entrance, giving a view of what should be a garden and half a street of red-brick workers' cottages now becoming fashionable. One of the men, who perhaps has foregone his session at the gym, has dark hair, a stocky build, and a face ruled by great, dark eyes framed by prominent lashes. The other is blond: but he is not a natural blond. He wears a white T-shirt with

sleeves ripped off. He has thrown a leather jacket onto the half-wall that edges the verandah. They haven't come to see me.

Monday 9 November 1992

I wanted to go see a show. Tickets were booked. The girls were going to come and pick me up. They did come. They waited. I couldn't get it together. I was too sick to go. I was too sick to go. I was too sick to go. I couldn't even talk to the girls. I couldn't do anything. I couldn't. I would like a nice muscleman to climb into bed with me and hold me, hold me, hold me tight. I want to go to sleep.

Wednesday 18 November 1992

Arturo would have been 23 today. And I would like a cigarette.

Friday, December 25, 1992
Marrickville, Australia
11:24 a.m.

Neil got out of the car and sniffed the thick air. This place was rich with the oily scents of the city, greasy to the touch and tasting of aluminium. The building looked no different from one he had been in fifty years ago. Red brick, squat, small windows, two-storeyed; unmistakably a hospital, even if this one went by the sanitised name of hospice. The other one, those years ago, had been awash with the smell of carbolic, but even that sharp odour could not completely hide the lingering trace of burnt flesh or the fetor of gangrenous tissue. Every time he came to this hospice he was struck by the difference of its aroma. Here, there was no carbolic pervading everything. There were no odours at all in the hospice, except those dirty, slimy ones emanating from the city. But even so, the ghosts of the airmen in that other hospital were here for him, their groans and their silences. The young men in this hospice in the hot, gritty Australian sunshine sometimes seemed to be the same young men he'd visited and frequently farewelled so many years past in that building in an English village.

The three of them took the goods they had brought from the boot and crossed the road. The shimmering heat rose up about them and caught in their throats. They paused to cough oxygen into their lungs at a little gate in the brick fence of the hospice. The gate opened onto a concrete path. This path separated the hospice from the larger institution of which it was part. The thin grey strip led up to a small verandah where a discreet sign announced 'Entrance'. To the left of the path lay a bed of wilting, blown roses, badly in need of a prune. This time Eileen had packed her pruning shears. It was very late in the season, but she was determined to do her duty as a gardener. An ivy-covered wall stretched up at the right. Somewhere not far away someone was playing Greek music very loudly, enough for it to reverberate off the high wall beside them and bounce the hectic rhythms amongst the sad roses.

Then a 747 roared overhead, taking off from the suffocating heat of Sydney for winter in Bangkok. A Thai Airways plane, carrying Christmas travellers to an only slightly less warm place. The noise of the jet made it impossible for them to hear anything else or to talk, so, with Neil in the lead, they set out up the path in single file.

Neil was carrying a great bunch of flowers they had gathered from the garden an hour before, and an Esky gently clinking. Eileen had a basket packed with biscuits, chocolates and fruit, Christmas crackers, chicken, ham and cake. Alex brought up the rear with four magazines, a bag of barley sugar and a paperback. That was all he had had time to buy on Christmas Eve at the Seven-Eleven on the highway.

It was just after 12.30. They had risen early, exchanged their little gifts to each other and eaten scrambled eggs, toast and mangoes. Hugo had slept under the breakfast table, passing wind. Now here they were in Marrickville, sweating even in the cool clothes they'd put on. They were coming to have Christmas dinner.

The glass entrance door had an automatic device attached that slid it open as they stepped onto the verandah. They walked through into the entrance vestibule and the door sighed closed behind them. The air conditioning immediately began to cool them. A small counter faced them from the opposite wall. There was no-one behind it. A large bowl of flowers had been placed at one end. The arrangement was spectacularly colourful, a vibrant kaleidoscope of reds, yellows, blues and white. Its natural beauty was in stark contrast to the pale institutional green of the walls, and the brown shiny lino on the floor. A little plastic Christmas tree stood at the other end of the counter, a string of lights on it flashing. Tinsel hung from the ceiling, and the front of the counter was bedecked with garish gold letters which spelled out 'Merry Christmas'.

A corridor opened off to the right, and they could hear, in the silence that had descended as the door had closed, footsteps approaching along it. A woman came out of the corridor. She had a little, red enamel badge pinned on her stylish yellow dress near her right shoulder, and a nurse's watch on a leather strap and a stethoscope hung round her neck.

"Neil! Eileen! Merry Christmas," she called as soon as she saw them. She had an accent, though not a strong one.

"Merry Christmas to you, Eli," Neil said.

"Merry Christmas, Eli," Eileen added.

"So this is Alex," Eli said. "How do you do, Alex. I am Eli Kalokerinos. Your grandparents have been here so often they are long-time friends now."

"Well," Eileen said, "all of you here have been very helpful in all this. I've brought something for the staff." She handed a present across to Eli. "It's not much but it might help those of you who drew the Christmas day shift," Eileen remarked. "How are things going?"

"Very quietly, Eileen. A lot of the boys who were well enough have gone to family or friends for the day. And the ones who are here, like Kieran, are no trouble at all. Thank you so much for this." She gestured with the present, which had the rectangular shape of a large box of chocolates.

"Shall we go in and see him?" Neil asked.

"Alyson would like to have a talk to Alex first, if that's alright. Kieran's sleeping at the moment anyway. He had a bad night. The morphine is doing its trick now though. Do you want to go down to the sitting room two doors down and wait for Alyson? I'll go get her."

They walked down the hallway to a room which opened onto the verandah. There was no-one in it. A plastic, push-button cafe-bar sat in the corner. But it was too hot for tea or coffee. There was a large Christmas tree in a corner of the room near a big-screen television, and a Coca-cola vending machine against the opposite wall near a small sink and cupboard. A bar fridge sat under the sink. There were a number of packages arranged under the tree. Whilst they were prettily wrapped, none of them looked like real presents.

Neil and Eileen sat down on a leather sofa facing the television. Alex took one of three armchairs. The armchairs were old, the vinyl and the faded remnants of once glaring colours suggesting they were contemporaries of the Beatles or the Rolling Stones. The sofa was much older, but either it had been made when furniture was meant to last or the years had treated it a little better. A laminate coffee table in front of the sofa was recognisable from a K-mart catalogue. They placed all the things they were carrying on it.

"I hope Alyson won't keep us here long," Eileen said. "The flowers need to be put into water."

"You could get a vase from the collection," Neil suggested.

"That's a good idea," she said, and she got up with the flowers and went over to the sink. She retrieved a glass vase from the crowded cupboard under it and filled it with water. She set the vase in the sink, unwrapped the flowers, and began to arrange them.

In the corner opposite to the Christmas tree, a card table held a pile of old magazines and some boxes of Pictionary, Trivial Pursuit and Scrabble. There were a few pictures of tourist scenes on the walls and a poster for safe sex beside the door; two naked men lying together on rumpled sheets. Alex could see it from where he sat, but it was not in either of his grandparents' lines of vision. He'd seen the poster before at a Healthy Living Festival Year 12 had gone to before the pressure of the HSC had put a stop to any other school activities. The poster had disturbed him then, and been the object of derision from two of his friends.

It was Mike who'd started it, after reading the poster: "Experience the pleasure of safe sex," he'd read, "yeah, for sure, experience doing it normally with girls, and that way it'll be a pleasure and safe."

"Experience putting on a condom and fucking some poofter up the bum." Vladimir had taken up the theme. "They say it's safe, but it doesn't sound like a pleasure to me."

"Do you want to experience the pleasure of safe sex, Alex?" Mike leered. He was holding up a condom, one they'd been given in a sample bag as they entered the Festival. "Turn around and drop your jeans and I'll please you with safe sex."

"Fuck off," Alex had replied.

"That's just what he wants to do," Vladimir hooted, "he wants to fuck off with you!" Vlad moved as if to grab Alex, as Mike struggled to rip open the condom pack.

Alex stepped back: "Both of you keep fucking away from me. Don't either of you touch me or I'll kick you in the nuts. Just leave me fuckin' alone!"

Vlad cooled it straight away: "Sorry mate. It was a joke, that's all. Meant nothing. Didn't mean to upset you. O.K.?"

"Yeah."

"But Alex," Mike was still intent on opening the condom, "you got me all worked up. I've just gotta experience the pleasure of safe sex with you."

"Well, you've left it far too fucking late Mike old bum chum. If you can't flick your dick out and into its rubber rain coat quicker than that you can't expect anybody to wait for you, can you? I'm gonna go and look for bigger thrills than what you can provide. But if you can get past the first step maybe Vlad'll help you experience safe sex." Alex had walked away. He found a toilet and washed his face in cold water in the basin. He combed his hair savagely, yanking a few strands out. He began to feel better. He avoided Mike and Vlad until they all had to board the bus back to school. Mike apologised then. But Alex ignored him. He sat by himself in a seat at the back and pointedly stared out the window all the way back to school. Though he knew he had to be careful. Silly fooling around like that shouldn't get him so upset. Otherwise the guys would start to wonder. The truth was bad enough without anyone thinking he was a poof too.

He tried to look away from the poster, but other pictures on the wall were worse. They all showed men naked, or nearly so, preening themselves before the camera. Alex turned his gaze to his grandfather, embarrassed that both Neil and Eileen were being confronted with these explicit images.

Neil had leaned his head on the back of the sofa, and closed his eyes. He could take these catnaps any time he found himself with nothing to do. Eileen was still fussing with the flowers, oblivious to the wall decorations. But something made her turn around to catch Alex's concerned look.

"What's up?" she asked.

"Nothing," he said, "I just don't like what's on the walls."

"The posters? They're a bit confronting aren't they? First time I saw them I was taken aback. But I don't mind them now. They serve their purpose."

"Yes," said Neil, quickly attentive, "though if I had my druthers I'd have the bodies covered up. Of course, they're not meant for me. Or you, eh, Alex."

"Not these ones, anyway," Alex said. Safe sex meant being covered up and protecting yourself. And protecting the person you were with too. But he would be with a girl. The guys on the wall, as fit and handsome as they were, did nothing for him. Did they? He looked at the poster again, wondering what he would do if he was in bed, naked, with a boy like either of those in the poster. Or maybe it was a matter of what either of them might do to him. Unless he were there, he realised, he would never know.

"Hello, Neil and Eileen. Merry Christmas." Alyson Ford invaded the room, mouthing kisses to Neil and Eileen. "And you've got to be Alex! I'm Alyson."

Since she was wearing an XXL, white T-shirt with large black letters printed on it proclaiming I'M ALYSON this seemed superfluous. The T-Shirt gave way to bright red tights, and her red hair was teased out in a halo around her head She had big silver earrings: elephants. Her red shoes looked more suitable for a dance floor than a hospice. But to show that she was in fact at work she had an official-looking folder and some forms in her left hand, and a pen in her right.

She flung herself into an armchair and the folder on top of the other items crowding the coffee table. She held onto the pen.

"You don't want any coffee? Can't offer much else Christmassy, though I'm hanging out for the bottle of champagne in the fridge. And a large gin and tonic! Come 2.30, that's what's going to go down my throat. Yummo! Speaking of which looks like you've brought enough to feed an army. Looks marvy! And I'm starving. Ravenous! Haven't eaten for days. But I don't think our patient will be eating too much. He's pretty weak. Though he'll be thrilled Alex has come. He's been talking about you, Alex, to everyone. So I'd better fill you in on how the place works. We're open for visitors pretty much all the time during the day. You can come in here any time for TV or coffee. Though that machine makes terrible coffee. I think there are cockroaches in the water heater. Probably in the coffee too. But it's better than nothing. Before we had that, visitors had to bring thermoses. Or bottles. Course a lot of them still bring bottles. To have a drink or two with the patients. Kieran likes scotch and bourbon. Did you bring any Neil?" Neil pointed to the Esky. "And wine. Actually most things alcoholic. We also let the patients smoke if they want to. Tobacco or dope, it doesn't matter here. So if you notice any funny smells, don't panic. No need to call the police. We just want everyone to be as happy and comfortable as possible."

Alex was reminded of the joint he'd forgotten in his pocket. He could have smoked it here. He didn't smoke very often. Since the HSC he'd had a few joints, mostly at parties with friends. One time the smoke had made him violently sick, perhaps because he'd had a few beers first. But usually he really enjoyed it. Laughing most of the time. Laughing at anything, and everything. He wished he'd taken his split of the deal from Vlad and Thommo.

"Alex," Alyson addressed him, "Kieran really wanted you to come and see him. Your grandparents have been visiting here ever since he was admitted, and they know all about him. But he's been gone from your life for quite a few years. Now he's back, really sick. How do you feel about it all? I have to ask for his sake. He can't take too much emotional trauma."

"I don't know. It's all so sudden."

"Are you angry with him?"

"No."

"Do you think he deserves to have AIDS?"

"No! But I do wonder why he didn't do what all the posters in this room were telling him to do."

"Well, I wouldn't wonder too much. It won't do anything for anyone."

"He could have kept quiet about himself, though," Alex said. "He didn't have to do it like he did. On Mum's birthday. He made such a big deal of it. It was no wonder that Dad got so angry."

'Yes, he could have done it quietly. He could have done it better, too, perhaps. If he'd known what he was doing. He was just feeling his way, learning how to walk really, and he got steamrollered," Alyson said. "But there are lots of things which might have happened that didn't. We have to deal with what did happen. We can't worry too much about maybes. Way back then, he was just telling you all he was gay. No big deal about that, eh?"

"Yes, there was. Dad couldn't cope with it. He went off the deep end."

"Has he finished his therapy yet? Is he off the bottle?" Alyson sat up straight, her eyebrows arched, her forefinger and thumb flicking the trigger on her pen open, shut, open, shut.

Alex flinched: "You know an awful lot about my family. What's all that to you?"

"Does it worry you that your brother is gay, Alex?" Click, click, click.

"It surprised me. He never seemed the type."

"Does your father seem the type to be an alcoholic?" The pen was silent.

"He's not. He just had a drinking problem. Leave Dad out of this." He returned her stare. She was too nosy for her own good.

"And Kieran doesn't have a gay problem. What he has is a viral disease. Let's not ask why or how or when he got it. Even if we could get answers we mightn't like them."

"I don't think I like any of this," Alex told the bossy woman lecturing him.

Alyson clicked the top of her pen against her teeth: "Alex, your brother has asked for you to come here and see him. You've come, so there is some feeling for him, right?"

"How sick is he, then?" His responses were heating up.

"Very sick. This place, it isn't for people who are likely to get better."

Neil gave a little cough: "This is a hospice for the dying, Alex," he said. A bloom fell onto the floor from one of the stems Eileen was arranging in the vase. They heard her whisper something to herself as she bent down to pick it up.

Alyson turned her attention to Alex. "Kieran hasn't got much longer. That's why he wanted to see you. He's taken himself off medication, as I've said. It's usually just days once that happens. Anything could take him off now. I'm sorry you have to get it all like this, Alex. If I could have done it any other way, I would have. It is going to be hard. That's one thing I can promise you. He only weighs about 30 kilograms now, so he looks a lot different to what you remember. And the chemotherapy has affected his hair. It hasn't all fallen out, but it looks pretty terrible. And there's an abscess in his mouth, in his upper jaw, that's pushed out his cheek. We can't control the infection there. So one side of his face looks like a football is sitting on it. He can't walk without help. And he's lost control of his bowels, so you'll find he's wearing a big nappy. And he's got pneumonia. But that's about all, I think, at the moment, apart from a few skin infections. I guess you can go see him now."

"Come on, Alex," said Eileen, "let's go see Kieran." She held the vase in front of her as she walked out of the room into the hallway, Alex following mutely in her wake. Neil picked up items from the coffee table and moved out after them.

Eileen led the two men down the hall, and around a corner. They could see into the room in front of them, the door of which was almost completely open. The sun angled in through half-closed venetians, dappling the covers on the bed, and the small mound under them.

A drip-stand stood up near the head, a tube snaking from the plastic bottle in it under the blankets, disappearing there. A small cupboard was on the other side of the bed. It looked like it was made of aluminium. It had a drawer at the top, then a door, which was open and showed two shelves. The top one had a CD-Walkman on it, with the earphones up on top of the cupboard, small black wires connecting the two. Crowded beside the earphones were five bottles of vitamins, two 250 mL cardboard packs of fruit juice with little plastic straws poking out the top, a paperback, and sunglasses.

There were two chairs under the window which an occasional rustle of the venetians showed to be open. Apart from that quiet noise the only other sound in the room was the wheeze coming from the shape under the bedclothes, a persistent though quiet enough rhythm emerging from an unseen mouth.

Eileen had entered first, and had taken the flowers up beside the bed where she was carefully putting them on top of the cupboard. Alex had entered slightly after her, but he remained unmoving just inside the doorway. Alex was perplexed. The shape in the bed could not be his brother. It was too small. His brother was big.

He took some steps forward until he could see over the bedcovers and make out the face on the pillow. He was right. It was not Kieran. This person was much older, much thinner, with not much hair, and a thin, straggly beard. The nose was a beak. And Kieran didn't have a great lump protruding from his right cheek, swelling the whole side of his face.

He began to open his mouth to say to Eileen they were in the wrong room, that this person was not Kieran, when the body on the bed opened its eyes. And uttered a strangled sound: "Alex".

"Oh," said Alex, "oh, Kieran." Then he was beside the bed looking down into his brother's face. Seeing close-up the sores on his neck and lips, the dry patches of skin on his ears and forehead. And the withered hands that emerged from the covers, the catheter from the drip sticking out of the right wrist. Kieran attempted to move it towards Alex, stretch it out for a handshake, but it palsied instead, and his twisted face contorted further in frustration and pain.

"I'm sorry to drag you down here, Alex," Kieran managed to choke out before he was racked by a spasm of coughing. Grey-green mucus dribbled out of his lips and down his chin. Alex stepped back, out of the coughing line. But Eileen moved in, in her hand a towel picked from the end of the bed, and wiped the drool from Kieran's face.

"Eileen?" asked Kieran.

"Yes, of course, it's me. And Neil's here too." Neil came into the room now, carrying as much of the food as he could. He moved forward into Kieran's line of vision.

"Hello, Grandpa," Kieran whispered.

"G'day Kieran, how're you going."

"I could be worse I guess, Grandpa. Someone could've poked me in the eye with a burnt stick."

"Or you could have been bitten on the funnel by a finger-web spider."

"Or I could have kangaroos in my top paddock."

"Or emus could've kicked your dunny door down."

"Yeah, all of that. So I'm not too bad," Kieran coughed, and his grandfather moved to wipe the phlegm which came out.

Kieran was weeping, the failing sight he retained blurred by tears flowing down his cheeks.

"No doubt you're drier that a dead dog's donger in the desert," his grandfather soothed, "but we've brought you something to wet your whistle. Let's just clean this up."

Kieran even as he coughed was trying to say something, tell them something. The three of them heard only a croak that was all he could force out now. Alex moved closer to his brother again and, with lead weights restricting him and time standing still, his chest constricting with what he hoped were not already spasms caught from his brother, dry ash in his mouth, sweat on his brow under his arms running down his back, he inched his arms across to take hold of his brother's hand.

His strong, healthy hand closed around his brother's skeletal, brittle fingers. And he held them gently, fearful any pressure would break the fragile shapes which had once been bigger, stronger, more powerful than his own.

Alex wanted to run away from that room, that body. Everything was telling him go, get out of there. But he stayed.

"What have you been listening to, mate?" he asked Kieran, with a flick of his head towards the Discman. "Hendrix?"

Saturday, December 26, 1992
Mt Kuring-gai, Australia
8:40 a.m.

Alex sprinkled sand across a seed tray. His grandfather rattled some wire against a tin behind him.

"When are you going to go back and see him?" Neil asked. Alex had dreamed all night of that little room in the hospice. He dreamed of the boy who was the captain of the school. And he dreamed of the misshapen, twisted body in the bed in that room in the hospice.

He had wondered whether he would be able to face the sight of Kieran again. Could he face seeing the wasted body, that grotesque face? Hearing the laboured breathing? Watching the shaking, yellowed hands reach for another cigarette, which would induce the hacking cough and strings of green phlegm? Like the hundreds before it, the cigarette would be stubbed out in one of the makeshift ashtrays always close to Kieran. And a few minutes later another would be lit.

Alex knew he didn't want to see that again. He wanted to stay here, sifting sand, preparing potting mix for cymbidiums. He just wanted to retreat into this comfort of his grandfather's orchids, and try to forget.

Try to forget Eileen saying to Kieran as he reached for another smoke: "Do you think those are very good for you, dear." And Kieran replying: "I'm not about to give up now. That'd be a waste of time, wouldn't it."

And Neil, tapping Alex on the shoulder, gesturing him out of the room where Kieran lay. "There are some forms I have to sign as the person responsible for Kieran. That's the term they use, but I want you to help me because we are both really responsible. If you were 18 already, it'd probably be up to you anyway. What Kieran has done is withheld his consent for further treatment. He's perfectly entitled to do that. I'm going to acknowledge that I agree with his decision."

"And that will mean he will die?"

"It will mean he will die faster. Do you know what I'd like to do Alex? I'd like to help him, give him something to help him slip away. Stop the agony. But we can't do that." The two of them were walking down the corridor towards Alyson's office.

"It's the same isn't it? Letting him not have any treatment?"

Neil was slow in replying: "The difference is it'll be very painful for him."

"How can we do that? Just let him die?" Alex could see only the stick figure in the room they had left. He wanted the strong young man who had left home in tears and frustration to come back and acknowledge all this was a mistake.

"Alex, you've seen him now. I know how difficult all this must be for you. But to prolong his suffering any more, that would not be an act of love." Neil had stopped and turned to Alex. He placed his hands on Alex's shoulders and spoke quietly and gently to him. "This is what he wants Alex. We are doing what he wants. And no matter what happens now, for Kieran only one thing is going to happen. He is going to die. Don't you want him to be able to do it as he wishes and with dignity? I've seen far too many men die in the most unpleasant ways with very little control over their means of death. Believe me, it hasn't been easy for all of us here to come to terms with Kieran's decision. It hasn't been easy for him to finally acknowledge all hope is gone. It's a very brave thing for anyone to do. I don't know if I could do it. So we must help him. Though God is on his side."

"God?" Alex blinked at his grandfather. "God didn't do this. I've read Kieran's notebooks. I know what did it."

"I do not ask God why it is so. If I questioned that, I would have nothing."

"How can you believe in God when Kieran is so sick, when you've been to war?"

"How can I not?"

They stood facing each other in the corridor, no more words slipping like secrets from them. For a long time they remained standing still, not looking at each other, or at anything at all. No-one came into the corridor, so they remained alone. Neil finally removed his hands from Alex's shoulders.

"Are you alright?" he asked.

"And you've been dealing with this for months," Alex said.

"Yes," Neil answered. They turned together to continue up the corridor. "I have really wanted to tell your father and mother. But Kieran wouldn't hear of it. He was concerned about you. Then, when Robert suggested you come spend Christmas at Mt Kuring-gai, Kieran felt you should know."

"I don't think I'm grateful."

Neil gave a short, grim laugh: "For what we are about to receive may we be truly grateful." And he knocked on the door they had come to.

Alyson sat at her desk with a cold cup of instant coffee and tired eyes. She was shuffling through a file to find the piece of paper Kieran had signed which indicated he did not wish further treatment beyond pain relief.

"We have to make sure we've covered all the bases," she said. "It's bloody awful, so cold and calculated, but we all have obligations here to fight for the living. Even when it's useless. This allows the doctors to issue not for resuscitation orders. Kieran has given his consent to the withholding of further treatment. We all think that he is perfectly competent to do so. Neil, if you could acknowledge that as the person responsible you agree with our view, and Kieran's instruction, we will have a neat and tidy file."

"A neat and tidy file!" Alex exploded. "Everybody is just signing him away."

"Alex," Alyson took up her cold coffee, "we are doing what Kieran has asked us to do. We are making sure that there can be not even the slightest doubt about Kieran's decision. Yes, we care about the files, because we care very much about Kieran and the rights and desires he still has left." She took a sip from the mug, then grimaced. "Ugh. This is awful."

Alex turned to his grandfather, who had just signed a sheet of paper agreeing that Kieran had withheld consent to treatment. Neil had taken off his glasses and was wiping his eyes with his handkerchief: "All we have done," the old man whispered, "is agree that Kieran still has the right to determine his destiny. We are doing only what he wants. God tells me this is the right thing to do."

And Alex tried to forget that, later, as he and Neil sat on the verandah with Eileen, waiting while Kieran had another of his naps, Neil had said: "Perhaps we'd better make a call to Bali." Yes, Alex had immediately thought, we'll get Mum and Dad home, and they can fix it, handle things. This was a crisis too big to be handled by him and Neil. His parents would expect their holiday to be ruined, now. Though they had said, please don't disturb us. Work out solutions if you have problems, this will the first time we have been away together since our honeymoon and we just want to be by ourselves. Be an adult. Besides you will be with Neil and Eileen, and your sisters are only a phone call away. But they couldn't have foreseen this. They would have to come back.

There was a rock pool. Anemones. Put a finger in the water. The angle changed. The finger became crooked. A bend in it. The hand further in. A bend at the water's lip. Finger down to an anemone. Shut! Another! A sweep of a hand over a rock of anemones closed the lot of them. A little fish. Hand grabbing for it. Again. Again. Again. The little fish darts and slips all about the rock pool but nowhere near the little hand grabbing for it.

"What are you doing?" asks big brother Kieran, his tanned body in a floating pair of board shorts, first a shadow above and then coiling down to join him at the rock pool.

"I'm trying to catch this fish," little Alex points, "but it's too fast."

"You'll never get it like that. You have to be quiet and secret. See, our shadows are on the water. Let's move to the other side. See, no shadow."

"What do we do now, Kieran? The fish is still too fast."

"Secret and quiet. Put your hand in the water and hold it still. Still. That's it! Just stay like that. Don't move. See. The fish is moving closer."

"It's coming right up. It's going to bite me."

"It might nibble."

"It is. It's nibbling my finger. It tickles."

"You could grab it now."

"No. I only wanted to touch it."

"That's good. It's too small to hurt."

The little fish stayed in the pool. And the big brother took the smaller one back to the umbrella and blanket where their parents were just beginning to be worried.

And Alex had asked Neil: "Does God think we should ring Bali?"

"Don't mock me Alex. I was thinking of your mother and your father, and what they would expect."

"Well, Mum and Dad didn't want to be disturbed. They specifically said to me to work out things for myself." He would have liked his parents here right at this moment, so he could leave all the decisions for other minds. The little fish he didn't want to hurt seemed to be floating upside down on the surface of the rock pool.

"You don't think they'd want to be here, Alex? They'd understand if we called them." Neil had come so far with the burden of his knowledge. In passing it to Alex, he could see some of his promises need no longer be honoured.

"Maybe they would. Or perhaps Dad will say it's typical of Kieran to ruin things. And Mum's always said what she doesn't know won't hurt her. They'll be back in two weeks, and they'll have had a good break. They'll need that won't they." The younger brother was not going to bring the older brother back to the safety of the umbrella. The umbrella had proved to be a false security.

"I can see the virtue in that. I'm not sure what good they could do here."

"No. That's up to us, isn't it, Neil."

The old man had glanced up from the magazine he had been flicking through. Alex was sitting in an uncomfortable hospital chair wedged against the wall in a tiny patch of shade. His face was turned to the floor, his hands hanging loose and still between his knees. Neil looked back down at the magazine.

"What do you want to do, Alex?" Neil had asked gently. "It was you Kieran especially wanted to see. You're the one he'd given the responsibility to for seeing things through. I'll do whatever I can to help, but Kieran has anointed you as his executor. That's what these bits of paper here say." He gestured down at a manilla folder on the floor beside his chair. "You just let me know what you want to do. I will help, but you are his brother."

"I don't want to ruin Mum and Dad's holiday. They were looking forward to it so much. And it was Kieran's fault, really, that they had so many problems over the last few years. I reckon Dad went off the rails when Kieran made his little confession. They deserve that holiday. I'll tell them that's what I decided when they come back." He hadn't looked at his grandfather. He had spoken the words quietly, head hanging. His hands had lost their stillness, silently wrestling each other.

"What about your sisters?" Neil liked the girls, though he had only known them on those rare occasions when Robert had succumbed to his wife's entreaties and asked his father and Eileen to a family function. He knew they were both practical, like their mother, though earnestly ordinary. They had accepted their father's dislike of Eileen and embellished it with a puritanical politeness which the virtuous reserve for second wives.

"They threw Kieran's clothes out in the street after him, Neil. I don't think he'd want me to have them come see him. He hasn't asked for them. He doesn't want them. He's still able to decide what he wants, anyway. And if I was them, I wouldn't want to come to see him. Doesn't he look awful." Alex whispered the last, a grudging admission of the truth they had all seen.

"He looks like a dying man, Alex." Since the truth had been admitted, there was no point in pretending.

"Have you seen a lot of them before, Neil? Like, in the war, I mean."

"I've been in hospitals like this before, and I've seen my share of dead and dying men. Burns are the worst. Horrible." He paused. There was a truth he had not allowed himself to admit, a dark knowledge that had snarled away inside him since his first night mission over Essen. This angry dog in his conscience had bitten away at him, each bite increasing the bronchitis and asthma that eventually led to him being transferred from combat flying. Fifty years later, he surprised himself by finding he was at last able to confess to his grandson. "Though I've done my bit in burning people, too. Bombing cities. Incendiary bombs. High explosive. There are some things you do because you don't have much of a choice about it. Sometimes you know you're doing the right thing, and you can be pleased with what you've done. Other times, it's not so easy. I'm glad I had a part in doing away with the likes of Hitler. That was right. But not all the people I dropped bombs on were Nazis. Children died. Women. Innocent people. If people can be innocent, that is. Some Christians say people are stained with original sin. I don't know about that. It's not part of my faith, anyway. I just wonder if there could have been solutions other than bombs and guns. That's the trouble with war. Too many people die for not much of a reason. And now we've got young Kieran here, soldiering on against a bug that's killing him."

Neil surprised himself with what he'd said. The words had come unbidden, but they had been always on his tongue, waiting. Years of silent witnessing finally reached an end.

"It must have been really hard, knowing all about Kieran, and not being able to tell anyone" Alex said. "I can't put it all together. He's so different."

"He's really the same," Neil answered. "What's different is now you share the secrets."

"I wish I didn't."

"Don't we all," Neil sighed. "If only we could unsee everything we have seen. But we are burdened with our memories."

"I wouldn't like to see burned people," Alex said.

Neil had not expected burns and fires and wounds. The farm boy had found the exhilaration of take-off an additional thrill to his new life as a trainee pilot. Emergency procedures were learned by rote, and guns were fired at targets, but it was all safely done in the familiar Australian landscape. It was when he left his birthplace and the world became foreign that the fun began to fade. Even before he had reached the Squadron in England he had found his hold on the world was weakening. What had seemed constant and whole began to appear changeable and fragmentary. In Colombo, the ship from Sydney had docked for food, fuel and water. The colonial authorities were keen to show off the splendour of decorated elephants and their pukka ways, so they invited the Australian pilots to afternoon tea with the white ladies of the town on the verandahs of the Galle Face Hotel. The maimed beggars on the streets reaching up for half-pennies and rupees shocked the newly winged Australians. And in a brief reconnoitre of the stinking town, Neil and five of the men with whom he shared a crowded cabin in the troop transport had nearly trodden on what they first thought was a sleeping beggar. It was only when Blue tried to rouse the figure with a nudge of his boot — they were keen to give this beggar some change since he was the first one who hadn't pestered them — that they realised the body was dead. Maggots trickled out of the mouth and nostrils and the six of them took off in a mad dash back towards the port and the safety of the troop transport.

In Alexandria, they had left the ship, and travelled by land to Cairo. They were there for three days: barracked in dusty tents; plagued by Arab children begging for money and food; assaulted by the dry heat and desert sand; affronted by the smells of a city without sewerage, electricity or running water; frustrated by the absence of women in the streets or on view; and continually enveloped by the sinuous discords of the music of Egypt. A keening ululation dragged them from sleep one morning, and they found themselves listening to the sounds of death. They were suddenly lost, no longer in a familiar world. And it became worse.

From there, they had flown through a dust storm from the aerodrome at Almaza in a Pan American Airways DC3 to Khartoum. A brief stopover revealed the Sudanese to them: tall, haughty, and very black. These great warriors stared disdainfully over the heads of the antipodean soldiers, who could not help being intimidated into the recollection of schoolroom lessons in Imperial history. They could see themselves beside General Gordon, assisting him in his futile stand against these giants in their animal skins. The young pilots shivered at the thought of sharp spears thudding into suddenly vulnerable white thighs, rib-cages and more sensitive parts. With equal shock, Neil recognised lepers, too, and saw signs of smallpox, and cholera, and other reminders that life here was not the dependable, unchanging routine of a dairyman-vendor in Maitland.

From the discontinuity of Khartoum, their plane had flown in short stages across Africa to land eventually at Lagos in Nigeria, where once again they spent several days bivouacked in tents, this time in the rain, with mosquitoes and leeches for company, and silent black faces continually appraising them.

There were drums in Nigeria, thumping rhythms accompanied by yelping voices. Neil was assailed by this strange cacophony as he lay awake in his tent, mosquitoes buzzing around the net, the constant patter of rain on the canvas above. Listening in the darkness to this music from another country, he'd felt himself drifting, and he thought that if he stood he would faint or fall over. The drums pulsed their rhythm through him.

He thought he recognised what music it was they were playing. He strained to hear the words the singers sang. He was sure he knew the song, and he would soon be able to join in.

But it was not his song. When the music ended it was still unrecognisable, though comfortingly familiar. He was in new territory, where strangeness passed for the ordinary, and where the everyday thoughts of an eighteen-year-old fresh from the farm were completely out of place. There were no familiar markers to guide him. His boredom had disappeared. Days were no longer a predictable, unchanging routine. He was just another face in this other place where few people were white, and the food something he would just weeks before have fed to the three pigs kept in a pen on the river side of the dairy. He slept on a canvas folding bed in a tent with three other men, and at some point yet to be determined he would board a ship to sail through torpedo infested seas so that he could take his place in a battle in the air. He had run away from the placidity of the routine of cows in one place to become a stranger in another.

He wasn't sure he knew who he was any longer. He thought he had forgotten his name. He lay in the darkness and tried to recall it. "I must know my own name", he thought, stifling the panic rising in him. "If I don't know my own name, I'll have gone mad." And his name slipped back into the place it had temporarily disappeared from. But he would remember, all through the years of fighting and after, when he had returned to Australia, the night he lay listening to music in a strange land and his name left him. The feeling that he was no longer himself, just some nameless being in a world of dubious familiarity, had never left him in a lifetime. He knew the fear of having nowhere you could call your own.

In 1945, he had come home to a land where the suffering was inconsequential compared to that he had witnessed. The women of Maitland complained that they could not get enough butter for their cooking, and the thick black beer of the Hunter was in short supply, but these were small imperfections on the surface of an ordered island, safe in its own ignorance of the wasted world beyond its shores. With his head full of three years' jagged memories, he was by then an alien in the land of his birth. It had become another country, with its music almost familiar but never again quite what he could claim as his own.

"What do you know about AIDS, Neil?" Alex questioned from his little patch of shade.

"What do I know? As little as I can, really. There've been a lot of things explained to us here about Kieran, why his immune system is collapsing so quickly, why he's had a host of infections through him, what sort of things he should avoid. We had a talk from one of the doctors once, when he was over at RPA, about how the virus replicated, invaded other cells and turned them into nasties. I don't want to know much more about it. I know more than enough now."

"It's funny that viruses like that are transmitted in semen or blood. Not like the flu, which someone can sneeze at you," Eileen said. Alex had thought she had fallen asleep, she had been sitting so still and quiet. "It makes you wonder about the bigger purpose of it all."

"You know all about that sort of stuff?" Alex was surprised his grandmother knew so much.

"What sort of stuff, Alex?" She turned her head towards him. He was difficult to discern, sitting cramped out of the light.

"How gays get it."

"How anybody gets it, I think," she said. "You can't get it from a sneeze."

"You haven't read Kieran's diary, have you." Alex didn't mean this as a question.

"It was for you only." Neil spoke for his wife and himself. "A gift to you from your brother."

"Dear, do you think you could get the ham sandwiches out of the Esky?" Eileen asked. Neil levered himself up from his chair.

"Kieran did some strange things, you know," Alex said, unmoving in the shade.

"Don't tell us any of it." His grandfather sighed and stretched. He moved towards the doorway. "I love ham sandwiches," he mumbled as he moved inside towards Kieran's room and the Esky.

"He's only recently opened up about the war, you know," Eileen said quietly. "It's been so long since then, and he's kept it all bottled up inside. He feels so much for Kieran. The other day he said 'they could have sent him to the Gulf War, or some Asian battle, or something. Shot him, or gassed him, or nuked him. No difference to what's happened to him.' I don't know myself. I'm not the believer your grandfather is. I'd have liked to have had my own children, but that wasn't to be. Your grandfather would say that was God's will. At least he would if you could get him to talk about it. But it was my body not God that decided. If I had been able to have children, I'd love them no matter what, and so long as they were happy they could do whatever they wanted to. But there's just Neil and Hugo. Though both of them do exactly as they please."

"Why do you think Kieran gave me his diary, Eileen? He's told me everything about himself."

"Don't you think that's the answer?" She adjusted her hat. The angle of the sun had altered. Alex's legs were no longer in shadow.

"But I don't want to know half of it."

Neil emerged onto the verandah. He had a plate in his hand, and he was stripping it of its covering of plastic film: "Kieran's awake," he said, "but just being cleaned up. A little accident. Ham sandwich, Alex?" He offered his grandson the plate.

Alex took a sandwich and bit into it: "Jeez! Hot English mustard!"

"I like hot English mustard and ham," Neil said as he offered the white bread sandwiches to Eileen. "Merry Christmas, everyone, again."

"We can have some wine when we go back in to Kieran," Eileen said. She took a small bite of her sandwich and chewed it carefully. "This is certainly a change to what we usually do. I suppose a change is as good as a holiday."

"Christmas is a holiday," Alex complained. He got out of his chair and moved over to where Neil sat with the plastic plate of sandwiches balanced on his knee. "Mind if I have another one?"

"Help yourself." His grandfather leaned back so Alex could reach the plate. "Every other year, Alex, Eileen and I have had Christmas morning to ourselves. It's become our custom. And if your father invites us over, we go there for lunch or dinner. But you know that doesn't happen too often."

"You'll remember this Christmas." Alex would himself.

"You're liking the mustard, then," Eileen noticed.

"It was just the initial shock. They're very nice sandwiches, Eileen."

"Only not really Christmas?"

"It's weird. I can't believe I'm stuffing my face like this, after yesterday and this morning."

"You have to eat," Neil said.

"Or you die," Alex answered. "But that's not what happened to Kieran is it? Maybe he should have eaten more and had less sex."

"No 'maybes', remember." Eileen wiped her mouth with a tissue and stood to brush crumbs from her skirt. "I'm going to see Kieran," she said, and walked into the hospice.

"In his diary, he writes about everything. It's disgusting."

"I don't want to know about it," Neil said. "The world is a big place, Alex, full of many different people in many different countries doing many different things. A lot of those things I don't do myself, either because I don't think it's a good idea or because I am completely ignorant of them. Some things, like eating a monkey's brain, are repugnant to me. But I don't think it is my place to tell other people what they should do. They may well think some of the things I do are pretty gruesome. I eat meat, for instance. A vegetarian would find that pretty awful. Actually, a bloke once tried to talk me out of being a meat eater. He had a pretty good argument. It was cruel to animals. Wasteful, because a living animal did more for the world than a dead one. Not good for the human digestive system because meat rots in your intestines while vegetables are quickly digested. A pretty good argument. But he also had halitosis of the highest order, and b.o. to boot. So many things are perfectly alright, but some silly busybody takes an exception to something and goes around trying to stamp it out. I don't go to church, but I don't want to go round burning down churches. I'm not a frequenter of brothels, either, but I'm perfectly happy for there to be brothels for those people who do like to use them. Nor am I a gambler, but I see nothing wrong with casinos."

"What he writes about just seems so dirty. I don't know how he could have done it."

"Life is essentially dirty Alex." The old man glanced behind him, to where Eileen had disappeared. "I guess you've never been with a woman at her time of the month. I'm not saying that's dirty, mind, but it can rather put a kybosh on the passion of the moment."

Alex was startled by his grandfather's admission of carnality. He had no image of aged amorousness. But Neil would have been referring to the past, perhaps Eileen, or it could have been his first wife, Alex's real grandmother. Or someone else, at any time at all: "Something to look forward to, then," he said.

"You dirty little bugger," Neil laughed at him. "I'm going to have to watch my tongue round you, aren't I."

Neil stood, and fastened the plastic film back over the plate of sandwiches: "Let's go see how he is." He moved towards the door.

Alex followed behind him, his head bowed with the responsibility that had been passed on to him. He muttered to his grandfather's back: "I don't understand how two guys can do that to each other. I always used to look up to Kieran. I wanted to be like him, you know. He was on the football team. He was on the cricket team. He was elected captain of the school. Everything he did, he was good at it. And everybody liked him. He could have had any girl at school. They were always hanging around him. Kieran was decidedly cool. Then he goes and blows everything by telling Mum and Dad he was queer. I still just don't understand it."

He heard Neil's sigh. The old man continued down the hallway: "We've gone over this. I think you'll find he felt so strongly about it he had to make it known. Some things are too big to hide."

"But why, Neil? Why would you want anybody to know you did things with other guys? Even if you liked it, you'd want to keep it secret so you wouldn't get the finger pointed at you." Alex whispered the questions to Neil, but his voice still sounded loud in the empty corridor.

His grandfather stopped and turned to Alex. The plate of sandwiches was held up between them: "Probably because he didn't want to hide it, and live a secret life. He obviously wasn't ashamed of it. Sometimes, you find you have to run against the world to be best able to express yourself. If we all conformed to what was expected of us, it'd be a boring old world."

"Well, you can be different and still be normal. Lots of guys are wearing ear-rings at school. And nobody cares how you wear your hair." Alex recalled he had tried to keep one haircut hidden, it had been so bad. His mother had insisted the barber do a neat short back and sides when no-one had hair like that any more. "Like, when I was in Year 10 we all had to look the same. You were a jerk if you didn't have the right look. One guy dyed his hair purple. He copped it for that, for sure. But being a poof — that's just too much. I couldn't tell anyone at school what had happened to Kieran. They all assumed he'd run away from home, which he did, of course, but no-one guessed why, because no-one ever thought he could be like that, except him."

"In this case I'd have thought he was the most important person." Neil was very matter of fact.

"But look where it's got him. He's here, dying. It's not that he didn't know about AIDS and safe sex and stuff. He did. It's almost like he deliberately got it."

"Alex, I think you're talking through your hat. Kieran has enough to cope with without you claiming he deliberately put himself at risk. You didn't see him the night he came up to us. He had tried to reach out to your father, to reach out for your father's help. Instead, that man, my very own son, turfed him out of the house and told him he was contaminated. Now, you're saying something a little similar. I can't stand for it. Don't you rob him of the little dignity he's got left."

"How did he know he was one? How do I know I'm not like him?" A haircut showed. But inside, where the blood flowed and the nerves tingled, what changed one man from another?

"I think you'd know. You'd feel different."

"Yeah, but different to what? Like, how would you know you're not normal if you think you're normal, and you don't realise everybody else isn't like that?" Alex realised he was almost quoting Kieran's words. And suddenly he understood why his brother had to publicly announce that he was gay.

"I don't know. I've never thought about it." Though the old man had lived with his own difference, the lost farm boy.

"But what did you think when Kieran told you about himself. It must have had an impact. You must have thought something."

"It's a while ago now, and we've had quite a few other surprises."

"But you didn't say 'hey that's great, Kieran, congratulations', did you?"

"No. I was a bit stunned. I didn't expect to hear that from him. Because I thought he was, well, normal. He always appeared as if he was, I can't think of any other word, except normal."

"Did you feel sick, thinking of him being with men?" Alex could feel the pimples on his chin reddening.

"I honestly didn't think of him being with anyone. He was very troubled. Your father had shaken him up a lot. He'd counted on his support. It was a revelation to him, your father being so against him. Yes, it was a big shock to him to suddenly realise he was from another country to the rest of us, when all along he'd thought he was a 'normal' type of bloke. I didn't consciously take that into account, but I knew he was lost. See, I've been there, in that lost space. It's like you're on the other side of the mirror. You can see through it like it's a window, but nobody can see you, and nobody can hear you screaming. You can't talk to anyone about it. But Kieran was talking to me. I was listening. I never talked about it. I just lived with it, on the other side of the mirror, in my own world, cut off. I left Molly, your grandmother, alone, you see. I shut her off because I couldn't talk to her. Why couldn't I, when here I am talking to you about it almost easily? You, not even an adult yet. But I didn't have the words then. Not with her. I was walking blind in my own desert, and I led her into her own, and she couldn't find her way out. My silence killed her. So I had to listen to Kieran, didn't I. Because I knew that dead agony of not being one of us, even if I didn't like the fact that he was one of them. Though there are worse things to be. He could have been me, with his grandmother's death on his mind, and cities of fire in his dreams. It was only that he loved men, Alex. Which is what Christ exhorted all of us to do."

"Not the way Kieran did." Alex almost laughed.

"No. Not exactly. But is that worse than butchering each other?" Or leather flight jackets on fire, limbs snapped into grotesque angles, intestines eviscerated by red-hot tracer? The white shadowless blaze of searchlights?

"You can't be blamed for what happened in the war, Neil. You had to do what you were told." Alex was suddenly conscious of the plate of white bread, with the pink ham and yellow mustard filling.

"That's the age-old excuse of the soldier. Yet we tried the Germans and the Japanese for doing what they were told. We still have war crimes trials. But war is the crime." Neil spoke very quietly, sadly.

"We wouldn't be free if people hadn't fought." Alex had written on the topic in his HSC paper. "Don't get me wrong, I'm really grateful you did, because it's one thing I don't have to worry about."

"War goes on all the time, Alex. It just comes in different forms. A guerilla war. Terrorism. Genocide. Or a virus."

"Are you saying Kieran's fighting a war?"

"His body is. He is, too, because he had the strength, or maybe the stupidity, to admit he was not one of us. He accepted his revelation. He didn't deny what he was."

"That didn't mean he had to end up here. He didn't have to be so stupid. He should have taken note of the risks." Then neither of them need be here, whispering too much of themselves over a plate of ham sandwiches. "Everybody knows them now."

"Are you judging him, Alex?" Neil asked. "That's a dangerous practice." The old man had been judging himself for over fifty years, and always finding himself lacking.

"He wasn't normal." It was the only word Alex could find. Even as it left his lips he wondered whom, if anyone, it could ever describe.

"He wasn't one of us, you mean. But Alex, what makes you feel so superior? Like I said, I have been on the outside, knowing I didn't fit in. Years I spent, living every day a life that was just the same outwardly as that of any of my neighbours. I studied, I got a job, I worked, I had morning tea with my colleagues, I came home and had dinner, I went to sleep with my wife, I woke up and did it all again. But inside I was an open wound, bleeding with guilt, and not even aware that my wordless pain sealed me in a cold heartland. I had to carry that secret world with me, my own burden. I could share it with no-one. I had to keep it secret, I thought, because I wouldn't have been a real man if I let anyone know my heartland was a horrorscape of fear, and guilt, and pain. How could I tell my wife I was guilty because I was alive, I had survived when so many others had died? How could I tell my workmates, who were proud of me for what I had done in the war, that I felt my hands were unclean and I was ashamed to have been responsible for so much carnage and destruction? That was my secret. It near drove me mad, and killed Molly. Kieran wouldn't live with a secret. He decided to be honest. I respect him very much for that."

"Are you going to go down to the Orchid Society or the RSL and tell them all you spent today seeing your poofter grandson in hospital where he's dying of AIDS?"

"Probably not."

"He had to know about safe sex, Neil. The whole campaign is everywhere. And he was in the top risk group. Why didn't he wear a condom, then?"

"I don't think we'll get anywhere asking that question. At this point it doesn't really matter does it? Yet I went off to war, no questions asked."

"But you weren't killed."

"No," the old man breathed out over the wilting sandwiches, "but there are times I think I should have been."

"Please don't tell me that. I want some help. He's my brother and he's dying and I don't feel I know him at all. I want to save him. I could have if he'd trusted me earlier. I wouldn't have let him catch the virus."

This corridor was fresh with summer air, antiseptically clean. Even so, Neil's nostrils remembered a similar corridor many years before where the sweet stench of burnt flesh lingered: "How, Alex?"

"I wouldn't have let him have sex. I would have talked to Dad. I could have got through to him. You and I could have, together. I wish Dad was more like you, Neil."

"The things we wish, eh. And your father used to wish I was someone else again. But we can't unscramble the past."

"If only Dad hadn't got so stroppy, if only he'd been off the grog then."

"Your father didn't mean to do this to Kieran, Alex. Nobody would have wanted this."

"I know that. Dad is going to be really upset. So that's why he should have a good holiday now. How come you and dad don't get along that well, Neil? I'd have really liked to have been able to spend more time together before this."

"It's times like these that you find out the most about people, Alex. A bit like going into battle." Neil found the words were surging out of him again. "People take on enormous burdens in an instant in war. Your father and I battled, but it was a skirmish, not a war. He blamed me for his mother's death, and then he blamed me for marrying Eileen after that. Your grandmother, she was an unhappy woman. I didn't realise how unhappy until . . . .

He had come back to Maitland, but the placid town was no place for his crowded head. The faces in the street spoke to him, but he could not interpret their murmurs. The belljar silence of dawn screamed him out of alcohol-fuelled sleep and into another jangled day, ducking for cover at ordinary bangs and ceaseless listening for non-existent engines in the sky.

Even back on the farm, he could find himself halfway through a conversation with his flight engineer, but with brother Harry's brown eyes staring at him over the head of a heifer.

There was a place he delivered to, with a daughter. She took to waiting for her milk. It might have been because once or twice he hadn't made it all the way around the town, some echo turning him another direction, and she was simply eager to have milk for her breakfast cup of tea. She needed her breakfast. She was a working girl. She worked as a packer in a clothing factory in West Maitland. She rode her pushbike over there at 6.40 every morning, except Sunday, when she went to church.

When Neil first saw her, she was standing in the kitchen doorway in her dressing gown, brushing her hair.

"We need eggs too, if you've got any," she said as he ladled a quart of milk into her billy.

The next morning, she stood in the kitchen waiting for the kettle to boil. She said nothing, but she was smiling. He knew now her name was Molly.

It was she who asked him to the dance on a Saturday night. It was she, too, who encouraged him to ask her to the pictures, and she kissed him first. She was also the one who tugged hesitant words out of him, as the thick blanket of his memories slowly unfolded. One evening they were out walking, the clear sky above them soft velvet sparked with stars. They sat on a bench and the silence sat down with them. Neil was staring up into the night sky. Suddenly, she realised tears were streaming down his cheeks.

"What's the matter?" she asked.

"It's very beautiful, isn't it," he said.

"Yes, it's lovely. And so peaceful."

"I'd forgotten that. The sky can be full of beauty and peace."

"You had to do it, dear. Don't get all upset about something you had to do to save us all from those Nazis and Nips. We wouldn't be sitting here looking at the sky if you hadn't done your duty. Something to be very proud of, that. I'm very proud of you for what you did."

"That it had to be done at all, that's what gets me."

"If every other man was as good as you, we'd never have any wars, would we? But the pity is there is only one of you."

And they were married in November 1946 at her church, with time for them to move to Sydney and find a house before he was to start his university course. The Government would pay for him to study agriculture, and once he'd finished there would be a position in the department. The least that could be done for those who had served. Though the discords still banged in his head. Mostly he had adjusted to the clamour, but, sleeping next to him, she soon discovered he spent much of the night awake, open eyes fixed on the ceiling.

They rented a small terrace in Enmore, just off Edgeware Road and close to the tram line to the university, and to St Luke's on Stanmore Road where she went every Sunday. He would stay at home and study though, as the cold months came on, he found himself in the rugby first fifteen and training on the university oval on Saturdays and Sundays. Their house was small, the bathroom with a wood-fired water heater in the backyard, and the toilet at the back fence so the can could be collected and emptied by the night cart in the back lane. There were rats in the open drains, and under the floors. Rats which would come up onto the table at night and roll precious apples and bananas onto the floor then drag them to their nests. The small thump of the falling fruit would fling Neil out of the bed and into the kitchen, where he chased the rats armed with a heavy frypan. Mostly he missed, but he had managed to club at least two of them.

Molly found a job in a shoe factory. The pay was poor, but it helped supplement the small allowance he received. And it took her out of the house and introduced her to new friends. Her girls from the shoe factory and his fellow students, mostly ex-servicemen like him but one or two younger ones, were a natural mix, and their little terrace a babble of flirtations on Friday evenings.

But then she found she was pregnant with Robert. She had to stop working. She began to be bored. Even after the difficult birth of the baby, which put an end to any ideas of other children, she was bored. But there was no thought of her working when she had a little child. Even though they had to mind every penny of the government allowance. Neil tried for some part-time work, but there were so many returned soldiers about, jobs were difficult to find. And any available were given to men, first, because now the men were back the women didn't have to work at all. Molly washed Robert's nappies in the old boiler, over and over again, even the clean ones, but there was nobody there to notice.

Neil never had time to notice, not for years. She'd withdrawn imperceptibly, at the same time as he had slowly brought himself back from the Europe of his mind and adjusted to being an Australian once more. Right through the fifties, he had shared a house, a bed with her and felt her go cold on him, but he hadn't known what to do. He is still unsure what happened. She had been so strong. . .

"Until what?" Alex had finally asked, his attention drawn to Neil's silence.

The old man turned and continued up the corridor towards Kieran's room, Alex beside him: "I was having to travel in the country every three or so weeks. I'd be away for a week at a time. I'd have to catch the train out from Central Sunday evening and sometimes wouldn't make it back till Saturday morning. Molly and I had a house in Drummoyne by then. I was working for the Department — I didn't ever work anywhere else after university — and if I was meant to be in head office that week I would travel into the City each day, my lunch in my port, and, when appropriate, my hat on my head. Home in time for six o'clock tea. In winter, the three of us would sit around listening to the radio, even later after television came. Because I didn't want to invest in a television until I knew it wasn't a passing fad. Robert'd do some homework, his mother would knit, and I might read the paper or a book."

"In summer we had another routine altogether. Robert'd be out with some mates cycling or playing cricket until there was no more light. I'd do some gardening. When I was out in the country it'd be different. I'd be booking into hotels and boarding houses, organising something to eat and the next day's travel, and having a beer or two too many."

"It was Robert who found her when he came home from school. I was in Goulburn, and I'd had to stay an extra day. She didn't know that. She'd have wanted me to be the one. Robert had to call the office in town, and the switch there called me and the police. The police got me back to Sydney that night. I don't understand completely why, even now. She wouldn't have wanted to hurt Robert. Even as sick as she was. These days, they'd have been able to help her. Some drugs or some counselling. Depression, they'd call it now. Acute depression. She'd become so unhappy. Her life seemed meaningless to her, and she couldn't talk to me, or anyone, about it. Mind you, these were strange things I didn't know about till later."

"That's how I saw it. Makes me wonder just what I see, but I'm still no clearer as to what I could have done about it. And temptation can be hard for a travelling man to resist. There had been occasions out in the backblocks when I hadn't been a faithful husband. But I was pretty sure she didn't know. She wasn't the sort who would have kept silent about it. They didn't mean anything to me except as a way of easing some loneliness. There was no-one I was about to leave her for. The whole thing hit me bad. I sold up the place in Drummoyne and moved north up to Mt Kuring-gai. I could still commute into the City. And the Department took pity on me and promoted me so I didn't have to travel so much. There still wasn't much time left to spend with Robert, and he needed time spent with him."

"Neither of us spoke much about it, then or later. Eileen came along and made me feel like a shipwrecked sailor finally rescued. Robert had to wait a few years until he started on his law course before he could be pulled out of the ocean. I know I should have tried harder. I should have comforted him more, been closer to him, talked about it with him. But I was broken, too. I didn't have the words or feelings for myself, let alone him."

"I'm sorry for you, Neil." Alex felt he had to say something.

"Don't be, Alex. I'm alright. Now. Your father, though I grieve over. What I've done! It seems a cycle, a mishmash of repeated mistakes. Here we are with Kieran, closing down all our feelings. Closing our mouths and minds, and taking all our hurt inside, where men bleed."

"Bleed, Neil? I thought only women bled."

"Women think only they feel all the pain. But bruises accrue inside a man, Alex. Dead blood, all around the heart. All the things we do and don't do because we've always got to look like men. At least Kieran broke out of the mould."

Alex reached across to his grandfather, whose eyes were watering, and put his arm around Neil's shoulders: "I don't want to be different, Neil."

"None of us do, Alex. That's why we keep our secrets, hiding our differences so that each of us is indistinguishable from the next man. Or so we think. And we remain filled with regrets. But it wouldn't be life if we didn't have something to regret, would it?"

Alyson appeared out of a doorway and waved at them: "I'm off shortly. Come by for a glass of champagne. I'm right about to pop the cork."

They had arrived at Kieran's room. Eileen had just come out of it. She had a green plastic bag in her hands. It was filled with clothes and towels for washing.

She smiled at her boys: "He wants to see you, Alex. He's nearly asleep. They tell me the morphine will keep him out for some hours. So you'd better make it quick."

"Well, then, after that I guess we might head off home and work out what we'll do tomorrow," Neil said "I'll start putting things in the car." The two men went into the room. Neil put the plate in the esky. He moved close to Kieran, whose eyes were shut. The old man reached out his hands and traced his rough fingers over his grandson's brow. Then he turned and picked up the Esky and a basket. He went out of the room again.

The hospice was by this time very quiet. As Alex had made his way to Kieran's room, he had caught glimpses through open doors of other men in their beds or seated reading or watching television. His eyes met the eyes of one, who smiled at him. He didn't smile back.

Kieran seemed to be already asleep. Alex was about to go when he heard his name being whispered. He went up to the bed.

"Hi, kid. I wanted to see you before I went to sleep. How's everything going? You finish the HSC alright?"

"Yep. All over. Just waiting for the results."

"You'll be o.k. Did you get those Nikes I sent you for your birthday?"

"Yeah." Alex was wearing them, but Kieran couldn't see that from his bed. "I'm wearing them. Thanks for those. Just what I wanted."

"I tried to always remember your birthday."

"You did. Every year. They were great presents too. And I never told Mum and Dad they were from you."

"You probably didn't tell anyone else either. Didn't tell anyone your poofter brother still gave you presents."

"What could I say, Kieran?"

"I know. I'm just pleased you got them and liked them." The effort of talking had caused mucus to dribble from Kieran's lips.

"I read your diary," Alex told his brother. He reached for a handtowel and wiped Kieran's mouth.

"And do you hate me?" The thin fingers fluttered on the sheets, and eyes dark in their hollow sockets looked up at the younger brother.

"No," Alex said, "I just don't understand."

"That's two of us then."

"I'm sorry, Kieran." Alex wondered if that was all he could ever say.

"Ah, mate, not half as sorry as I am. But I really need you round. I'm ready to go now. Will you be here for me?"

Alex said nothing.

"Alex?"

"Yeah. I'll be here." They were very difficult words to utter, especially as he meant them.

"I've given you all that's left of me, Alex. It's not much, is it."

"It's a lot, Kieran. I'll never let go of it. And I'll never let anyone else read it. You'll be safe with me." There was a movement in his chest, as if blood were congealing in a dark bruise near his heart.

"I didn't want to hurt Mum and Dad, Alex. Or you. Or anyone."

"I know. So we won't tell them anything at all. It will be our secret." Alex picked up a small towel and wiped some drool from his brother's chin. Kieran smiled. At least, Alex interpreted the facial contortions as a smile.

"Could you do something for me?" Kieran asked. "Put the earphones on me. I like to drift off listening to music."

"Here we go. What do you want to listen to?"

"There's a CD there. 'Something to sing about'."

Alex picked up the CD cover, opened it and placed the CD in the machine. The cover had cartoon characters on it, two men and two women. The men were together, and so were the women. Little cartoon red ribbons showed on their cartoon jackets.

"Can you start it at 'Rubber Duckie'?"

"'Rubber Duckie'? Like from Sesame Street?"

"Yeah. I like that one."

"What is this CD?"

Kieran was quiet, listening to the silly words of the song, then he whispered: "It's music from my country, Alex."

In a few minutes he was asleep, and Alex had left.

So, when his grandfather asked in the dust mote filled light of the greenhouse "When are you going to go back and see him", he hadn't had to think. He would be back again today. He had promised Kieran.

Monday, January 4, 1993
Mt Kuring-gai
3.17 p.m.

Neil removed the bottle of Bell's from the paper bag. He placed the bottle on the kitchen bench.

"What'll you have, dear?" he asked Eileen. She was already bent over the sink, scrubbing and peeling potatoes she'd just retrieved from a dark corner cupboard.

"A gin and tonic, thanks. A strong one, I think."

Neil turned to face Alex. He was seated at the table turning over and over a pair of sunglasses.

"A scotch, Alex?"

"I don't drink it," Alex started. Then, "But I might start. Yes, please."

"With water and ice?"

"However you have it."

"Ice. A little water." Neil proceeded to open cupboards for glasses and the gin and tonic. The fridge for cold water and ice. Slowly, deliberately he made up the drinks. He passed the clear one to Eileen.

"Here you go, Alex, wet your whistle with this." Neil took a sip of his own. "I think I need this one."

"It's best, isn't it," Eileen said above the rush of water from the tap. "He was in a lot of pain. And he knew his mind was not like it used to be. The way he reached for a word, and he couldn't remember it any more, looking so bewildered because he had never had trouble like that before. And all those sores and things. He was such a handsome boy."

"That probably never did him much good," Neil grunted.

"What do you mean?" Alex asked.

Neil had his glass raised halfway to his mouth, but he put it back down: "Maybe if he'd been uglier we might still have him with us, like he used to be. He mightn't have been in such demand. But I don't know. He knew what he was doing. Though I'd have liked to have seen him out of that world, with those people. Some of them are nothing more than brain washers."

"Who?" Alex cautiously raised his own glass and sniffed it.

"I don't know who. But I do know Kieran is now dead."

The hospice had phoned early in the morning. Kieran had stopped breathing at about 4.30 a.m. and pursuant to the patient's instructions, there had been no attempt made to resuscitate the patient. The patient had been heavily sedated and would have felt no pain. The death had been certified by the resident medical practitioner, and the hospice was about to notify the undertakers whom the patient had selected in anticipation of his impending death. Would the family care to attend the hospice to collect the patient's effects? It would be preferable that any viewing of the body be negotiated with the undertakers. The hospice had sealed the body in accordance with its standard practice and was awaiting its collection. The staff of the hospice extended their consolations to the family with regard to this unhappy event.

"What's that got to do with brainwashing?" Eileen turned from the sink and took a sip of her gin. "Do you think someone talked Kieran into getting that disease? They'd have to be a pretty good talker."

"No. But I reckon Kieran started off really well. He was a good, honest kid who recognised there was something a little different about himself. I can understand that well enough. I can understand it only too well. So I think Kieran did a gutsy thing by facing it head on and saying to himself 'well, no sense in living a lie'. I've seen blokes who live lies like that. They hang out in public toilets and are just basically obscene. It's a sex thing. And those guys are often married with kids. I don't understand how they can go home all dirty from whatever they've done in a public toilet to kiss their wives and play with their children. That's a real problem for me. Of course, two blokes would never have been able to shack up with each other when I was young. No, that's not true. I remember a few blokes who shared rooms or a house. 'Unlucky bachelors' mum used to call them. They'd be labourers or oddjob men. I used to wonder how they got by, you know, for a sex life. They could have been doing it with each other. And, you know, that doesn't worry me so much as the idea of these ones in public toilets."

"Why? Because the others are doing it in secret and hiding it from everyone?" Alex was savouring the smokey scotch."No. Because they're caring about something, each other even."

"But who says Kieran was so angelic?" Alex said. "He knew what he was doing." The diary had been intruding itself into his dreams, and sometimes it wasn't Kieran in the strange fantasies, it was himself.

"I don't care what he did," Eileen said as she filled a saucepan with water and placed it on the stove. "He was a lovely boy. Lovely."

She turned the element on and moved back to the bench where she began to dust veal cutlets with flour.

"Isn't it a bit early for dinner?" Neil asked. Eileen turned to look at the clock on the microwave.

"Yes, of course it is." She bustled over and switched off the stove. "I don't know what I'm thinking of." She came over to the table and sat down with Neil and Alex, her gin and tonic in her hand. "I'm all muddled."

"I don't know what to do," Alex said.

"I think it has all been done," Neil said. "Alyson and Kieran made sure everything was organised."

Together, the three of them raised their glasses and slowly sipped their drinks. Under the table, the old dog farted.

Friday, January 15, 1993
Kingsford Smith Airport
Sydney, Australia
7.41 a.m.

The Qantas flight from Denpasar was due in at 7.50 a.m.

Alex and Neil had been up at 5.00, and washed, dressed and breakfasted by 6.00. Eileen had declined to make this particular excursion.

The night before, both Tracey and Lisa had separately called to check that the return of their parents had been remembered.

"I'm so sorry you have to go so far, Neil," Tracey had said. "If I could have spared the time I'd have gone in. Just as well you're retired, isn't it, so you have plenty of time on your hands."

"I do hope that Alex hasn't been a lot of trouble for you," Lisa told Eileen. "Mum and dad were so disappointed with him before they went away."

"He's been no trouble at all," Eileen said. "Do you want to talk to him?"

"No, not really. Wouldn't know what to say to a seventeen year old boy. I'm sure they only have sex and hormones in their heads."

"I think Alex has a little bit more than that in his," Eileen had replied.

The trip down to the airport had started off well. They had a quick trip down the freeway as far as the turnoff to the highway. But there, the traffic had soon increased and it had been a slow trek from Gordon down to the Harbour tunnel. Once they were through the stream which mostly terminated in the City, they had a better run and were able to find a parking spot quite close to the terminal. Inside, Alex scanned the monitors: "It hasn't landed yet. But it's still showing on time. They're supposed to come through Gate A."

"Right. We'll watch different ends of the exit. I'll take the left and you take the right. That way we shouldn't miss them."

The international airport was busy. Numerous planes were coming in after the night curfew. A steady flow of people emerged from the doors of the Customs Hall. About five minutes after they had arrived the monitor changed to show the flight from Denpasar had landed.

"It'll still take a while for them to get through customs," Neil said. "About half an hour." But it was only twenty minutes later that Alex saw his father's familiar figure come through Gate A. His father was pushing a trolley with three suitcases on it. His mother was following him, carrying her handbag and two airline bags. She wore a sarong knotted at her waist and a loose white blouse. Alex waved at them and they both waved back, and pushed through the crowd at the barrier to where Neil and Alex stood. Alex was engulfed in his mother's big hug. Her perfume spread in a wave around him. His father shook Neil's hand, then Alex's. Robert was wearing shorts and sandals, and a batik shirt. He reeked of aftershave.

"How're you going?" he said.

"Fine," Neil answered. "You have a good holiday?"

"It was wonderful, Neil." Alex's mother let Neil take the two airline bags from her. "Perfect weather. A beautiful hotel." The four of them moved to the exit, the trolley squeaking all the way. "And fabulous food. I must have put on three or four kilos."

"It doesn't show, Mum." His mother flashed Alex a smile. They were outside, crossing the road into the Car park. It was noisy and hot.

"I've got a present for you," she told him. "I hope you've been good for Neil and Eileen."

"No, Mum, I've had drug dealers delivering heroin and I've got a plantation of dope growing in Neil's greenhouse."

"So that's what those plants are," Neil played along.

"There have been no problems then?" Alex's mother asked Neil.

"With Alex? None whatsoever. The weather's been a bit crook though."

"Yes," Robert said. "It's as humid here as Bali." They had arrived at Neil's Commodore and Neil opened the boot.

"Alex, you'd just love Lombok," his mother was saying as the bags were lifted into the car. "And the girls on Bali are so pretty. You'd really like them."

Neil had unlocked the car and was reaching across to lift the lock on the passenger door. Robert got in beside him and Alex and his mother took the back seat. She reached in her handbag and brought out a small package.

"Here you are Alex," she said as she offered it to him, "it's duty-free from the plane. Aramis. We've got more things in the luggage."

"Thanks." Alex examined the little box of aftershave. "This should stop me smelling."

"Oh, stop it Alex. You don't need to make fun of everything." His mother smiled at him. "I'm so tired. The plane didn't leave until nearly 10.30 last night, and I didn't get much sleep. I'm looking forward to getting home and having a nap."

"We were down at Turramurra yesterday," Neil said. He was rolling down his window to pay the parking toll. "The lawns are mowed."

"Thanks, dad," Robert said. "There was no need to do that."

"I didn't. Alex did."

Robert turned in his seat to face his son: "That was good of you. Seems like you've turned over a new leaf."

"I've seen the light, dad. I've treated you and mum so bad. I have to make amends."

"No more drugs," Robert warned.

"No sir. I'm in rehab. Totally pure."

"And what else have you been up to while we've been away?" his mother asked.

Alex started to take the plastic off the box of Aramis: "Nothing much," he said.

Wednesday, January 6, 1993
Rookwood Cemetery
Sydney
9.47 a.m.

Neil, Eileen and Alex almost lost themselves following the street directory from Mt Kuring-gai to the western suburbs. The green expanse of Rookwood stretched across a page, seemingly unmissable. Neil, thinking he knew a shortcut across Parramatta Road, had taken a wrong turn left off Concord Road. It had been a long time since he'd driven in the area. He'd forgotten a new expressway had been built. They ended up in the new sports centre, none of which showed on Neil's rather antique UBD.

"This has got to be it," Neil unnecessarily said as they rounded another semicircular drive following the neat white signs to the non-denominational section.

"You don't think we're going too fast, dear," Eileen wondered.

'We're right, we're right," Neil answered, though the car slowed perceptibly.

"We don't need to rush," Alex said from the back seat. "It isn't as if anything is going to happen until we arrive."

"Thank you, Alex." Neil said. "That's good plain sense. I'm getting too edgy. We all have to try and keep our heads. This is going to be tough."

"I think we might be close," Eileen said. "The next left is the one we want."

"Great!" Neil breathed.

"Kieran told me he'd invited all his friends," Alex said. "I wonder what they'll be like?"

"He invited people to his funeral before he died?" Eileen asked.

"He couldn't do it once it had happened, could he?" Neil said. "Anyway, it wasn't as if it wasn't going to happen was it. Just a matter of ensuring those you want to remember you, can come. Most of us don't get the chance for that. Lot of blokes I know would have liked that. We used to joke about what we'd say at each other's funerals when I was in the air force. We got the opportunity pretty often too."

"Don't dwell on the war, dear. This is 1993. It's nothing like war now. All of that terrible stuff is over. We've been a country at peace for over fifty years. You don't need to bring up all that old stuff."

Ten thirty had been the time they were supposed to meet Alyson Ford and the few other friends paying their last respects to Kieran. It was

10.28 when Neil, expletives suitably restrained for Eileen's benefit, pulled into a tarmacked parking lot.

It was raining. A steady drizzle. Eileen had an umbrella, a sombre dark blue, matching her smartly tailored dress and shoes. She hadn't wanted to wear black.

Neil was wearing a jacket. The moth balls which had protected it for the twenty or so years since he'd last fitted into it had stunk the car out. It stretched too tightly across his big back, and wouldn't do up around his stomach. His white shirt had been ironed that morning by Eileen and was remarkably free of garden dirt, rust or sawdust, though he'd taken a stroll in the back garden whilst she was touching up her perfume. He'd found an old tie, navy blue, very plain. His formal black shoes had been pinching his big feet from the moment he'd put them on. They had some mud on them. He hoped they wouldn't have to walk far. But at least no-one would notice the mud with the rain coming down.

Alex had no tie, no jacket. He was wearing what he considered one of his best shirts. Eileen had almost spoken to him about it, her first thought that orange and blue were not the colours for a funeral.

But she had reconsidered, and had pinned an orchid to each of them. A small, slipper orchid. Hers looked just right on her dress, the delicate white accentuated and amplified against the dark colour. Neil's lapel bore his flower well, too, but the jacket demanded full attention, squeezing Neil in, and pulling his shoulders back so he walked with a sailor's roll. Alex's shirt almost overwhelmed his spray. But he had brought a big bunch of flowers as well, mostly orchids, though Eileen had also picked the best blooms from the garden that morning.

Alyson had seen them arrive and came running up as they began to look for a track to follow across the wet grass.

"We're over there", she waved at the small group of people some 200 metres off. Umbrellas were up. The group was out in the open on a mowed green area. To reach them they passed over little bronze plaques set into small, flat pieces of concrete. Rows of them. They followed one particular row. As they walked towards the group, no further conversation necessary, it was obvious a grave had been dug. A pile of earth, wet clay, was partially covered by a piece of artificial grass. Another piece of the green plastic grass covered the hole in the ground.

"I'll try for introductions," Alyson smiled apologetically at Neil and Eileen, "but it's a difficult time for social niceties."

"We understand perfectly," Eileen answered. Both Neil and Alex were silent. The group they had become part of was about twenty in number. Apart from Alyson and Eileen there were only three other women. One of them had a shaved head, and a ring through her nasal septum. She also had numerous rings and studs in each of her ears. The other two women stood separately, slightly apart from the group. One wore a linen suit which she was protecting with a white umbrella. Alyson introduced her first. She had worked with Kieran. The third woman was smoking, also under an umbrella. She had a pram with her, the pram too swathed in protection against the rain for the baby to be seen. She had lived in a flat next to Kieran, until he had had to move into the hospice. The woman with the shaved head was introduced only as Ramona. Then quick and confused introductions followed with the men.

They were a variety, some in their forties or fifties, most in their twenties. Some were wearing raincoats while others had umbrellas. A few were obviously couples.

But everybody there was happy to meet the three of them. There were kisses and hugs for Eileen and handshakes and pats on the back for Neil and Alex. A table had been set up under a beach umbrella. The table had a red and white checked cloth on it, and there were bottles out, a tray of scones, some pate, quiche, dolmades, oysters and chips.

A man approached to offer them each a glass from a tray. "I'm Vaughan", he said. He had a rich melodious voice. "I'll be doing the reading. Kieran asked me quite some time ago, and I said yes. But he didn't tell me what he wanted me to read. I do hope you won't be shocked."

"Shocked?" Again it was only Eileen who spoke.

"He's asked for a couple of poems to be read that are, well, a little erotic and homosexual".

"If that's what he wanted, I'm sure we'll be able to cope with it." It was Neil. "We mightn't fully understand or fully approve, but a man's got to sing his own song after all. Kieran did that. We don't want to slight that in the least."

"But please take a drink, Neil," Vaughan said. "Kieran requested that we serve a good malt at the graveside. He was partial to a good malt."

"So am I, so am I." The grandfather's voice was croaky and scratchy. He grabbed a shot glass from the proffered tray and upended it down his throat. Eileen moved her hand around his free arm, and left it linked.

"Will either of you speak, Neil? Alex?" Alyson Ford asked. "Vaughan will read, but we thought we should say a few things before that. If one of you were to start things off, we might just go round the group and let anyone who wants speak."

"I think Alex should speak. I won't," Neil said.

"I don't know what to say," Alex said.

"Just something about him," Alyson suggested. "Whatever comes into your head. I've found that's often the best way."

"He'd told me he didn't want any religious service," Neil said to her. "I more or less took that to mean he didn't want any ceremony at all."

"There won't be. An exchange of memories, that's all."

Over on the road a long, white hearse had glided to a standstill. Four women dressed in white got out, and opened the rear. They slid the coffin out of the back. A worker cleared the artificial grass from the hole in the ground. Two poles were left spanning it and a long flat cord was placed across each one. The white ladies each took a corner of the coffin and carried it silently over to the grave. They rested it on top of the poles and stood back, a little apart from the rest of the group.

Alex stayed near Alyson as the onlookers moved to form a circle around the grave. Eileen stepped forward and put her orchids on the coffin. They stood in the rain, watching the drops fall on the polished wood of the coffin and the delicate flowers placed on it, and alone with each other. Vaughan began to read. There were two poems. The first was only three verses long. The second took a little longer. The group stood in silence.

Then Alex spoke: "My brother was really good to me. He looked after me when I was little and always remembered my birthday. On June 2 this year he would have turned 23. I will remember his birthday, but I'd have liked him to be there for it. I am going to miss him, because I guess I loved him."

Ramona said: "Kieran was a real good mate and great fun to be with. I remember him at Mardi Gras, having a fanstastic time with Arturo. I hope they are together now and having fun."

A young man being hugged by another young man said: "I wish we didn't have to say goodbye, Kieran. We'll always remember you and your smile."

And the voices continued around the circle until it was Eileen's turn. She said: "We love you, Kieran."

Neil said nothing. But he reached inside his jacket and took out a small medal, dull bronze, with a flash of ribbon. He bent down and placed his Victoria Cross on his grandson's coffin.

The group stood again in silence. The white ladies moved to the graveside and took up their positions at each corner. They raised the coffin slightly, using the cord. The poles were slid out, then they began to gently lower it into the ground. The flowers and the medal disappeared from view. Once the coffin was in place, the poles were put back and the artificial turf was placed back over.

Vaughan began to pack the bottles and food from the table into a basket. Other people strolled away into the rain. Alyson gave Eileen a kiss and shook Neil and Alex by the hand.

Neil, Eileen and Alex meandered over to the car. As they were getting into it, they heard the engine of a small back-hoe start. It moved to the pile of dirt near Kieran's grave and scooped some up and deposited it in the grave. There was more mechanical noise. Another scoop was poured into the grave.

Neil started the car and put it into drive.

Thursday, 25 April, 1996
(ANZAC Day)
Turramurra, Sydney
4.45 a.m.

Alex had set the alarm for well before dawn. He had got up in the dark, dressed and left the house while his mother and father were still sleeping. He had driven into the city. After the kilometres of sleeping suburbs, he was pleased to find signs of life there. The movement he saw was mostly old men, and others not so old, moving from all directions towards Hyde Park and the Cenotaph. He had to manoeuvre around the road blocks to reach East Sydney but once there he found it easy enough to park that early in the morning. Once he'd locked the Volvo, it took him only a few minutes to cross over to Hyde Park.

In the car he had pinned the miniature row of Neil's ribbons on to the left breast of his shirt. He had all the medals, bar one, at home. Neil had left them to him.

He found that the little piece of cloth which took precedence in the small bar of colour on his shirt set him apart from the men and women he walked amongst. The quiet murmuring of old friends greeting each other in the not quite light paused as old eyes recognised the ribbon on Alex's chest. The old eyes were set in lined, sagging faces. The faces were attached to stooped, gnarled, slow bodies. But these bodies still made way for the young man who had come amongst them wearing the sign of the bravest, the most honoured. Alex was ushered in unanimous silence through the crowd until he stood in front of the steps to the Cenotaph, beside the dark Pool of Remembrance.

Then it was dawn. The single bugler played the Last Post. The crowd of rememberers cast their eyes to the ground. Above their heads, the lonely flame in the Cenotaph continued its eternal flicker.

After the dawn service was over, Alex drove slowly back to Turramurra. He had no wish to stay for the march. Neil had never marched.

His parents were awake when he eased the car into the driveway. He went first to his bedroom, where he put the row of ribbons back into the medal box. The box now also contained a black covered notebook with a red spine. A name was written on the right hand corner in silver ink. He had read what was in the notebook only once. But he would never part with it, any more than he would the medals and ribbons. The notebook was his own secret. He was the only person alive who knew what was in it. He didn't need to read it again to know that his brother, like his grandfather, had had a life. Neither of these lives were for him, but the secrets that had been shared were part of him, and so he was linked in more ways than just blood.

He made his way from his room down to the kitchen, which was warm and bright, its east-facing windows spilling in the Anzac day sun. His mother was preparing scrambled eggs and toast. His father was grilling tomatoes and mushrooms, which he was preparing to serve with fresh rocket.

"You'll have some?" his mother asked. She had already set three places at the table, and fresh orange juice waited for him in a large, dewy tumbler.

"Yes, please. It looks great. Why all the trouble?"

"We just felt like it. We woke up and thought 'what would be a good idea'. Then we started listing the things we liked until we came up with a menu for the things we had."

"How was the dawn service?" his father asked. He had finished with the mushrooms and was now smearing Vegemite on his toast.

"Very simple. Very peaceful. I was glad I went."

"I always get sniffy when I go to those sorts of things," his mother said. She pressed the plunger on the coffee.

"Are you going to go every year, now?" his father again. "Dad never went, you know. He never liked to remember the war."

"I know. I just wanted to go this once. Because Neil really cared a lot about the mates he'd lost. Though he'd never talk about it much."

"It beats me how you can know so much about the old bugger. He never talked to me about any of that sort of stuff. And I was his own son. What did you do to end up getting on with him so well? He was such a moody bloke."

"Robert," his wife reproached, "don't speak like that about him. He wasn't such a bad thing. He obviously had a bad time of it in the war."

"But that was over fifty years ago. You'd have thought he'd have been able to get over it in that time."

"He was a really good man, Dad," Alex said. He licked some traces of orange pulp from his top lip. "It hurt him that he ended up a hero and lots of his mates ended up dead. He lost three commanding officers in a couple of years, you know."

"Did he tell you that?" his father shot at him. "He never discussed any war things with me."

"No. I read it in a book. When I got his medals. I wanted to find out."

"Robert, you sound like you're jealous of your father and Alex. Leave it be."

"I'd have liked to have known him a little better, that's all. At least we managed to talk civilly in the last couple of years. He seemed to try with me. But he had a lot to make up for. He basically drove my mother to her death." Alex reached for a slice of toast. He slowly, deliberately spread it with butter. The little notebook was stowed away in the medal box with its story. Therefore, his father's own truths were safe. Alex was the guardian of the secrets that could challenge them, but Alex could see no point in confronting his father with other truths.

"That's something that happened a very long time ago, Robert. You don't really know. The poor woman needed help, for sure. But would your father have known that?"

"I was surprised the ribbon was so recognised," Alex said, leading his father back to safer ground. "It's so little. If it had been the medal ..."

"I can't believe that the big medal is missing," his father interrupted. His mother reached for the coffee pot and began pouring for the three of them. "It's not as if Victoria Crosses grow on trees. What can Dad have done with it?"

"I'm sure Neil has put it in a safe place," Alex said. He had never once heard his parents mention Kieran's name since their second honeymoon. They seem to have expunged him from their memories. "Anyway, he didn't really care for it. He didn't consider himself the bravest of the brave. He said the ones who were dead should get the medals. It was enough to have survived."

"My father said that? That's a very lovely thought."

"That's why I went in this morning. I thought I could take him to his mates, wherever they are. Each one with his own God."

His mother started: "God, Alex? Has young Libby been having a talk with you about the good book and its place in your life?"

"No, Mum. Just because her parents have become Pentecostal doesn't mean she has. Though they want her to be. It was Neil who talked about God."

His father stopped chewing his toast: "Dad? Talked about God? What on earth did the two of you get up to while you were gardening?"

"We just chatted."

"Dad never went to church. Ever." Robert could remember Sunday after Sunday when his mother had dressed him in his cleanest shorts and whitest shirt and taken him by the hand to church. There he had had to sit on hard pews and kneel on bare knees while his father had stayed at home reading the paper.

"Because he believed the house of God is within each person, and each person has his own relationship with God. So you don't need to go to church because you can always talk to God."

"I don't believe this. Dad had a relationship with God and he talked you into believing with him?"

"No, I don't believe any of that. I'm an atheist. I think, if there were a God, why does he need to be so cruel? But Neil believed God existed within each of us, and so all of us could speak directly to God, and therefore we would each have our own God." Alex wasn't sure whether Neil had actually voiced these thoughts to him. Perhaps he had just absorbed the old man's philosophy along with tea and dirt under his fingernails.

"This is too much for me on a holiday. Especially at breakfast. Really, Alex, for someone who won't be twenty-one until June you have developed a very heavy turn of phrase." Robert slowly shook his head and reached for his coffee, which he gulped.

"It is Anzac Day, Dad. Lest we forget and all that." Alex took perverse pleasure in exploring the limits of his father's patience.

"Give us a break. You're sounding like some type of zealot. By the way, are you still going up to see Eileen today?"

"Yes. Libby and I are going up for lunch. And I'll see what Eileen needs doing up there. The lawns probably."

"I'm surprised Libby's parents will let you go out with her alone," his mother noted. "Given their very interesting religious views."

"You'll have to take your mother's Volvo," his father continued. "Your mother and I want to go and see a movie."

Just after eleven, Alex pulled the old Volvo up to the kerb outside Libby's house. He checked his appearance in the rear-view mirror. His hair was still neat. He'd worn a cream shirt with an Oxford collar, but he'd drawn the line at a tie. He had teamed the shirt with black slacks, black socks and black shoes. But he'd packed clothes more suitable for physical labour in his gym bag. He started up the meandering concrete path that led to the small verandah and Libby's front door. She opened the door just as he stepped under the verandah roof. She pushed open the flyscreen door to show her shy smile. She was wearing jeans and a long-sleeved cotton top. She carried a denim jacket and her bag in her left hand, and her keys in the right.

"I'm ready," she said. "You look very dressed up. You must have expected someone else to answer the door." She turned to lock the door.

"There's no-one else here?"

"Mum and Dad are out at an all day prayer meeting. Praying to save the world from sin. Too much sex. Too much debauchery. Not enough repentance."

Alex relaxed a little. Libby came up to him and they kissed. He put his arm around her shoulders and they turned to stroll towards the car. Her head rested briefly on his shoulder and he could smell herbs which would have to be from her shampoo. There were always delightful little mysteries to her like this that he was unravelling.

"I'd have thought a day like this might have encouraged prayers for world peace," he suggested.

"World peace, no, that was one of the slogans from their last transformation. I liked it better when Mum and Dad were Trotskyists, you know," she said. "They did make me go to the youth group, but some of the kids in Resistance were almost fun. And Mum and Dad were a lot calmer and more together when they were against solid things like exploitation of workers and apartheid and nuclear testing. But then communism died, and they couldn't hack it any more. I really hope they grow out of this Christian phase soon. With luck the next change might turn them into nice, ordinary suburban parents like yours."

Alex opened the door for her, and she got in. He moved around to the driver's side and sat down beside her.

"My parents live in a sort of cocoon," he said. "They refuse to see a lot of what goes on round them."

"And mine don't?" Libby asked as he started the car and pulled out onto the road. "Mine create their own world to convince themselves they are changing it. They have this drive to do good, whether as evangelical Trotskyists or Pentecostal Christians. They insist on doing good, whether anyone wants it or not."

"Mine wouldn't do anything that might get them known as being a little strange. They want to be exactly the same as everyone else in Turramurra. They want to be normal." Alex turned on the radio.

"I love this song," Libby exclaimed as the sugary arrangements of a Mariah Carey song filled the car. "She has got such a great voice." Alex hummed along, and with other tunes until he pulled into the driveway of the house in Mt Kuring-gai.

Eileen was pulling some weeds in the front garden. She levered herself out of the cushioned support she used when she needed to get down on her knees and slowly progressed over to greet them, purposefully exercising her arthritic joints. She reached Libby first.

"How are you, dear?"

Libby bent to give her a kiss.

"Fine, Eileen. It's just so nice to be out for the day and not have to work."

"Yes, it's good to have a holiday in the middle of the week."

Alex had come up beside Eileen and he too reached down to give her a kiss. She asked: "How was the dawn service?"

"Moving."

Yes. I was thinking of you then. I was up that early. It was very good of you to go and represent our heroes." She smiled at him, well aware of the secret they continued to share.

"Eileen, it was the very least I could do." He didn't really know what he had done or why he had done it. He had not planned to go to the dawn service. It had simply seemed the proper thing to do.

She patted him on the arm: "You're a good boy, Alex."

"I can see your lawn needs cutting," he said moving away from her and bending down to inspect the untidy grass. "Do you want me to start on that now?"

"Lunch won't be ready for a bit, so if you wanted to, I'd be very much obliged. Libby, don't let me pressure you but there are some things you could help me with in the kitchen."

"No problem," said Libby. "I love watching how you cook."

The two women walked arm in arm up the drive towards the backdoor. Alex opened the boot of the car and took out his gym bag. He followed the women, but passed where they had entered and continued on into the yard. He strode up through the ankle deep grass to the old shed where the mower was kept. He pulled open the door and stepped in. He dragged clothes out of the bag and quickly changed into shorts and a T-shirt. Old gym boots replaced his patent leather shoes. He eased the mower out into the sunlight and attached the catcher. He checked the fuel and throttle, then pulled the starter. It spluttered into life. He adjusted the throttle down and pushed the mower across the lawn so that he could begin mowing parallel to a garden bed. Halfway along the bed he passed a white cross, with Neil's neat black painted letters on it: "Here lies Hugo, beloved companion. xii.3.1993."

"You silly, old fartbottom," Alex muttered, continuing to push the mower up to the end of his first row.

A Note on Sources and Background

In researching the historical events referred to in this fictional work I have relied on both oral and written sources.

My information on the air battles over Germany during World War II comes from: *Pilot's Flying Log-Book* of Flying Officer A. Fisher, D.F.C., B.V.S.C. (Sydney), R.N.Z.A.F. (he was attached to R.A.A.F. 467 Squadron) and from forty years of conversations with him; *Australians at War: In the Air 1939–1945*, Volume 1, Ross A. Pearson, Kangaroo Press, Sydney, 1995; *The War in the Air*, Gavin Lyall (ed.), Hutchinson, London, 1968; and *Units of the Royal Australian Air Force, A Concise History. Volume 3, Bomber Units. Volume 10, Chiefs of the Air Staff, Aircraft, Bibliography,* compiled by the R.A.A.F. Historical Section, AGPS Press, Canberra, 1995.

Details of life in Maitland and the day-to-day existence of a dairyman-vendor were kindly recounted to me by Ron Austin. Other information has been gleaned from local histories, oral recounts, and ephemeral sources.

Information on HIV and AIDS has come from a wide variety of both medical and general literature over many years, as well as from anecdotal and ephemeral sources. No one source can be nominated as a basis for my writing as the impact of the epidemic on my own life and the lives of very many of my friends has been profound. The accretion of this knowledge was not asked for: it happened as a matter of course.

I have taken technical information on informed consent and not for resuscitation procedures from *Nursing and the Law*, 3rd edition, Patricia Staunton and Bob Whyburn, W.B. Saunders/Bailliere Tindall, Sydney, 1993, but the view portrayed does not purport to be a legal one. I am grateful to Professor Megan-Jane Johnstone of Royal Melbourne Institute of Technology for conversations and discussions on the ethics of caring. Her own publications in this area are unsurpassed.[1]

Dr Peter West of the University of Western Sydney has been one side of a dialogue carried out over a number of years with regard to relationships between men. Whilst this dialogue has influenced some of the thematic development of this work of fiction, I do not fully subscribe to Dr West's essential argument. However, useful concepts appear in his work *Fathers, Sons and Lovers,* Finch Publishing, Sydney, 1996.

There were two Australians awarded the Victoria Cross whilst in aerial service in Europe in World War II. Wing Commander Hugh

---

[1] Johnstone, Megan-Jane, *Bioethics: A Nursing Perspective*, second edition, W.B. Saunders/Bailliere Tindall, Sydney, 1994; *Nursing and the Injustices of the Law*, W.B. Saunders/Bailliere Tindall, Sydney, 1994.

Edwards, serving with the R.A.F., received this supreme distinction for his bravery over Bremen, Germany, on 4 July, 1941. Flight Sergeant Rawdon Hume Middleton was similarly recognised for his courage in returning a plane from a mission over Turin, Italy, on November 28, 1942, and allowing his crew to parachute to safety, after which he turned the crippled plane and crashed into the sea. This story concerns neither of these brave men. My creation of a third awardee is a piece of fiction.

As this is a work of fiction, the reader should not suppose that I have interpreted actual historical events without licence. I have instead used history as a source for threads with which to weave this particular story. It is true, for example, that there was a raid on Remscheid on July 30, 1943. The events recounted here, however, are entirely fictional though viewed through this historical framework.

Acknowledgments

Michael Hurley (especially), Glenda Adams and Graham Williams at University of Technology, Sydney have been extremely supportive in their patient, wise criticism. Rose Moxham, Pamela Freeman, Ian Harman, Anna Phillips, Lorraine Bennett, Anne Sahlin and Ron Austin read and commented on some or all of the many drafts. Julie Sweeten at the UTS Library provided much assistance in identifying the odd sources I was after.

Dr Margaret Bradstock of the University of New South Wales and Bruce Sims of Magabala Books were excellent examiners.

Lloyd Christison has provided support and encouragement throughout and this work would not have been completed without him.

www.ingramcontent.com/pod-product-compliance
Ingram Content Group UK Ltd.
Pitfield, Milton Keynes, MK11 3LW, UK
UKHW020126250726
13967UKWH00002B/506